About th

I HAVE BEEN INTO CREATIVE WRITING FOR MORE YEARS THAN I CARE TO REMEMBER AND HAVE DABBLED IN MANY GENRES. HOWEVER, I HAVE ALWAYS BEEN FASCINATED BY 'TALES WITH A TWIST' AND IN THIS HUMBLE COLLECTION I WOULD LIKE TO THINK THAT I HAVE ACHIEVED SOME MEASURE OF SUCCESS. WOULD YOU AGREE? THE ONLY WAY TO FIND OUT IS TO READ ON

Derek J Rogerson

25 assorted tales with such twists that one would think they had been written with a corkscrew whilst descending a mile high helter skelter in the teeth of a whirlwind. However, they all contain a common theme dear reader and unless your imaginative thought processes are as convoluted as mine, at the conclusion of each you will undoubtedly whisper under your breath, 'Well I never saw that coming.'

Dedicated to my family for their unflagging encouragement and to Sue my number one fan.

CONTENTS

A terrifying werewolf with a tooth brace, bottle-top glasses and wearing an 'Alice Band'? You've got to be kidding me. Well not really – They certainly do exist out there somewhere. For further details why not read on and perhaps you just might recognise somebody you met in some nightmare or other!

Gimee the Moonlight---------

There was something eerily beautiful about the full moon in winter. The way it would sneak in between the trees at 5'o'clock in the afternoon. This time of night though there was no such distractions as passing cars or people walking their dogs. At this time of the night it was the perfect setting for the werewolf fraternity, especially the timid ones like Cruel Fang and me.

I mean Cruel Fang! Go on! What sort of a mental image are you getting? One of a creature that's all hair and teeth, with wild staring eyes and a temperament to match? Huh! You couldn't be more wrong. Sure enough, all the aforementioned attributes are present – in spades, except that the hair is held back with an Alice band; the teeth are restrained with a quite formidable brace and the wild staring eyes are peering myopically through bottle-top spectacles.

Mind you, he has a nice roar. It's a pity about the lisp though. Somehow 'wwwhooarr' instead of 'RRRHOOARR' doesn't quite conform to the usual macho image of a fully paid-up werewolf.

But I digress. Cruel Fang and I are abroad this chilly winter's night as we are on our 'final warnings' from the WWF. No not the wrestling thingy. I'm talking about the 'Worldwide Werewolves Federation'. Terribly exclusive of course. Normally only werewolves with attitude are allowed to join. Luckily for us CF, as we all call him, has an uncle in high places that pulled a few necks for us and got us admitted as VW's. No! Not the car silly, 'Virgin werewolves'. You know, never ripped a bodice open or torn of an arm or a head in anger. Ughh! I cringe just talking about it.

Oh! We went to all the meetings, even took part in some of the less gory ceremonies, but after 50 years on the VW benches, even the more understanding members of the federation were beginning to wonder at our lack of commitment. Then that fateful day came. We were summoned into the presence of the Master werewolf and told, in no uncertain terms, that unless we started some

serious bodice ripping, coupled with limb mangling, then we were for the 'bullet' – silver of course.
However, we were not thrown completely to the wolves (sic). Bludenguts, the Chief training officer had arranged a number of observation field trips where we could pick-up, first-hand, the finer points of limb mangling; brain crunching and heart ripping. What we were also allowed to 'pick-up' after the usual carnage was the odd arm or leg that had not been completely devoured; the residual spilt brains and as a special treat, the occasional heart or two that had been missed in the mayhem. It certainly beat the pre-packaged stuff that CF and I normally picked up down at Bodyparts-R-Us – and totally organic as well!
The field trips were reinforced by visits to local cinemas that still occasionally had showings of the old Lon Chaney and Bela Lugosi horror films. Bludenguts had hoped that us seeing the somewhat scaled-down interpretations of werewolf activity would give us a taste for the real action. In truth though, apart from the bodice ripping, we were usually quite terrified. We were even thrown out of the 'Roxy' during one matinee performance when CF, forgetting where he was, screamed out 'Thame – thame' when poor old Lon got his 'come-uppance' in the final reel of 'Curse of the Wolf Man'. I'll never forget the screams of terror (CF swears to this day it was laughter) expressed by that usherette as she threw us out yelling, 'If you've got to dress for the part – try and make it look a bit more realistic.'
But of course all that is behind us now as we crouch in the bushes on this cold winter's eve', waiting for our first victim. The Master has decreed that unless we return at

dawn, drenched in blood; our teeth dripping brain tissue and with an internal organ clutched in each hand then we had better not return at all as we would, without doubt, be banished to some far-flung, desolate corner of the land. Oh! Dear. Imagine the ignominy and disgrace that would be heaped on us by such a sentence. Never in the history of the werewolf fraternity had such terrible words been uttered. Well certainly not since 1342 when it transpired that a distant relation of mine, Braingorger, had turned out to be a vegetarian. Banished to Millwall he was along with Hellsbreath, the first werewolf closet cross dresser. Unfortunately for him they found his closet full of carefully washed and ironed ripped bodices they did. Rumour has it that their ancestors made good though – yeh! Almost humanised they were and apparently the majority of 'em can be found most Saturdays, cheering on the local football team!

But wait! CF clutches my shoulder and points with a hairy finger at the couple that are approaching our hiding place. I note that they are both females of the species, with bleached blonde hair; bright red lips; mascara daubed heavily around their eyes and wearing short leather skirts; white high-heeled shoes and, believe it or not – bodices! (Actually, they're what are now called boob tubes, but hey, why get semantic at a time like this).

As one, we spring from our place of concealment with blood-curdling screams and confront the 'ladies'.

'Cor! You boys are a bit impatient aint you?' says the taller of the two 'ladies of the night'. 'What'l it be then? A short time or back to my place?'

'I want your heart - PLEATHE' roared CF, his thick glasses slipping down his hairy nose.
"Ere that Mandy! This ugly 'airy one 'ere wants me 'art! - I'd go for the usual bits darlin' if I were you, it'l work out cheaper.'
'No no! I inthitht. It mutht be the heart.' Responded CF politely, his talon tipped paws reaching towards the snow-white bodice (sorry! Boob tube).
Now Tracy, being a fully paid up member of the 'oldest profession' was, or so she thought, wise to all the tricks of the impatient punter, wanting to 'do the business' prior to fiscal negotiations. But here was this smelly, four-eyed, hairy creep, badly in need of a manicure, trying to actually paw the 'goods' before any mention of recompense.
With a lightening move she struck him across the face with her shoulder bag, filled with a multitude of bulky items. This included the princely sum of £69.50, mainly in fifty-pence pieces donated by an earlier 'customer', who had just dropped the jackpot at the 'Trousered Ferret' and was most happy to share his good fortune, after favours received, with the peroxide duo.
I flinched as the bag struck CF high on the temple. I winced when a split-second later her stiletto heeled shoe crunched sickeningly into his groin. Oh! And I also fled when Mandy moved threateningly in my direction.
The ladies dusted themselves down, applied further layers of 'lippy' and mascara and headed off to richer pastures. As they passed me crouched behind the dustbins, I heard them laughingly compare their latest contretemps with a recent incident concerning a group of Millwall supporters.

I hurried back to where I had so ignominiously fled from CF's side to find him nursing his head in his hands, muttering something about wishing he'd been born a vampire.
'Never mind,' I said. 'The nights still young. We could get lucky yet.'
I think we both got the scent at the same moment. Yes, it was definitely fresh human blood. If there's one thing that us werewolves are good at it's detecting the distinctive aroma of fresh human blood. And there it was – in spades (or should that be hearts?), hanging pungent in the cold night air. CF and I stood with our arms around each others shoulders, sniffing the crisp air deliriously and looking for all the world like fugitives from an 'X' rated advertisement for a certain brand of gravy granules.
We quickly ascertained the source of this delectable scent and realized it was coming from the local Church hall. It was then that the penny dropped. We had stumbled onto a blood donor session. I felt quite despondent, yet this initial feeling of despair was quickly dispelled as CF told me of his cunning plan..
CF put the large Blood Transfusion Services van into gear, slipped the clutch and we were off. Hurtling down the High St with at least fifty crates of delicious human blood to be consumed at our leisure. It was every werewolf's wildest dream comes true.
When I think back on this crazy escapade, I realize that letting a shortsighted werewolf loose on dark city streets, in a van containing booty that he couldn't wait to get at, was not a particularly good idea. Now don't get me wrong! I'm not pretending for a moment that I would

have taken the corner any slower. Neither can I truthfully say that I would have braked before the van went straight through the butcher's window, ploughing through an assortment of freshly slaughtered beasts, before finally coming to a standstill in about a ton of offal waiting for disposal.

CF says I really shouldn't have laughed when I sat up to find him covered in blood from the smashed bottles, with an assortment of hearts; livers and lights festooned around his broad hairy shoulders.

'You weren't a pretty sight yourself,' he said, a smile playing round his thick warty lips, exposing his awesome teeth brace.' But then again I suppose all's well that ends well.

I don't think I'll ever forget the expression on the Master's face when we burst into that initiation ceremony.' I nodded sagely. 'That poor initiate! Never even seen a bodice – never mind ripping one open – and there we were, blood running of us and forming puddles on the temple floor. You with a pig's heart in one hand and a sheep's brain in the other and me with an assortment of livers and kidneys draped around me. Mind you I was lucky to get rid of the string of sausages I spied hanging from your tail. I think we might have had a problem explaining them away!'

Yes, all that was years ago but it certainly proved a watershed for the modern werewolf movement. So impressed were the hierarchy at our perceived bravery that pretty soon after the momentous event, CF became the new Master and I was elected Chief Training Officer. In the ensuing period we have managed between us to change the direction of the brotherhood. These days there's very little limb ripping or head crunching and I can't remember when I last saw a heart torn from a bosom.

Still, some traditions are easier to forego than others and at each full moon CF and I can still be found ripping open the odd bodice or two. I suppose however that it's some latent urge passed down from the days of Braingorger and Hellsbreath that makes us love our football. We've just been accepted as honorary members of a supporters' club. What was that – which team? Why Wolves of course!

No doubt you've all seen the commercial. You know the one I mean. The one with the gigantic ethereal hand, hanging in the sky, with a ghostly finger pointing at the next lucky Lotto jackpot winner. Now be honest! How many of you have, perhaps just for one fleeting moment, imagined that the finger was pointing directly at you? Yea! I know; we've all experienced that particular dream. And then reality kicks in as you realize that at odds of nearly 14 million to one, the hand may as well be

displaying the adjacent finger as well, cocked in that age-old symbol of defiance.
However Nathaniel Longbottom thought processes did not run along the same lines of the rest of us mere mortals, who have been blest (or should that be cursed) with the gift of logical reasoning. Why even the initials of his name matched the National Lottery. This could not be mere coincidence and in his mind that finger was undoubtedly pointing at no one else but him. To say that the lottery had become something of an obsession with Nathaniel would have been an understatement.
From day one he had unfailingly staked far more than he could afford in an effort to find the elusive 'six'. Every Wednesday and Saturday night would find him perched on the edge of his chair, his many tickets spread out before him as the presenter announced the winning numbers for the draw. Needless to say, despite repeated checking of his tickets, he was never able to match the elusive half dozen. But Nathaniel, after perhaps a twinge of initial disappointment, dismissed each successive failure with profound stoicism, convincing himself that the next draw would be the one.
Meg, his long-suffering wife, had long since given up all hope of convincing him that he was chasing a dream. A dream that over the years had gradually attained nightmarish proportions as more and more of his hard-earned salary as a postman found its way into the till of the local lottery shop. The day she found out that his weekly outlay exceeded the grocery bill was the day she realized that there was now only one love in his life and it wasn't her. And so she packed her bags, walked out of the

house that many years ago he had changed the name from 'Mia Casa' to 'Camelot' - and left him.
Nathaniel, philosophic as ever, looked on her departure as a favourable sign as he realized he could now devote more of his time studying the logistics of the mystical forty-nine numbers; ever searching for a pattern or sequence that would lead him to his ultimate goal and happy in the thought that when the win did come he would no longer be required to share the millions with her.
Despite spending all of his free time with his great obsession, Nathaniel did not neglect his duties as a postman. He of course realized that his income was important in order to finance his all consuming passion and he considered himself fortunate that the nature of his work still allowed him time to muse about what he would do with his new found wealth when his numbers came up.
However, on this particular Wednesday morning he was shaken from his reverie as he gazed intently at the letter he had just pulled from his postbag. The reason for his bewilderment was due to the fact that although he was familiar with his delivery round, staring out at him from the manila envelope was an address he had never heard off '3 Guinevere Alley'. He knew there was a Guinevere Road but 'Alley'; this was a new one on him as he scratched his head, totally baffled. Reason however prevailed and he assumed that it was probably a narrow passageway that ran off either the 'road'. However, he thought it strange that in all the years of delivering in the area he had never been called upon to visit this particular address.

Nathaniel had walked the length of the aforesaid road without any luck and he was just about to consign the missive to the 'dead letter' section of his bag when right at the end he spied an extremely narrow opening displaying a sign that proclaimed that this indeed was the elusive Alleyway. As he turned into it he realized that as well as being narrow it was extremely short, containing just four dwellings; three ancient looking cottages and what appeared to be a rather dilapidated newsagents shop, which also happened to be number three. He searched without success for a letterbox in which to post the letter and had little choice but to deliver it to the addressee in person.

A bell above the door announced Nathaniel's presence in the apparently empty shop. While he waited for attention his eyes were drawn to the well-stocked newspaper rack where he spied the daily paper, which he generally picked up from his local newsagent at the end of his round. As he scanned the front-page headlines there was news of a disturbance at a protest march through the town on the previous day. 'Funny' he thought to himself, 'I thought that was planned for later today. Must have got it wrong.' It was then he noticed the date on the paper – Thursday 11th. Now he was confused. He knew damn well that it was only Wednesday as he had still the lottery tickets to purchase.

Minutes passed and still no one appeared from behind the dark damask curtain that separated the dimly lit shop from the living quarters. Nathaniel by now was sorely intrigued with the newspaper that appeared to have been printed a day early. He waited a further couple of minutes before leaving the letter prominently displayed on the counter along with the exact money for the strange newspaper, which he carefully placed within his postbag.........

Nathaniel completed his round and eventually reached the town's main street where he observed his usual end of shift routine of calling into 'Mick's Coffee House' for his daily shot of caffeine. He remembered the strange newspaper in his bag, which he now took out and began to read. He got no further than the second page and was surprised to see what he assumed were the previous Saturday's Lotto results. Closer scrutiny however revealed that they carried today's date. He looked closer at the numbers displayed and soon realized that they certainly were not those for the previous draw. A lump formed in his throat and his heart leaped as he quickly scanned the remaining pages to see that he was looking at news that was yet to happen.....

The cynic within him assumed that this was an obvious hoax. Someone with an overactive imagination was having a laugh. He smiled to himself as he finished his coffee and proceeded to follow the rest of his Wednesday ritual; that of purchasing his lottery tickets.

"£59 Nat" said the young shop assistant as she handed him his tickets. As he handed over the three £20 notes he suddenly remembered the six numbers he had seen in the 'hoax' newspaper.

"Forget the change Sue," he said to the girl as she held out the £1 coin. "Make out another ticket for me with these numbers." Nathaniel had only seen them once but each one was etched clearly on his mind's eye.

As fate would have it, Nathaniel had fallen asleep in his armchair that evening and had missed hearing the Lotto results. It was the following morning before he saw them and as you have no doubt deduced, his final ticket purchase matched with all six numbers. He had often thought as to what his reactions would be if this was ever to happen and yet strangely enough he felt perfectly calm as the realization dawned on him. All he could imagine was how right he had always been about the oversize finger that really had been pointing at him.
As he contemplated the millions that were to come his way, a sudden worrying thought clouded his initial euphoria. How many others was there that had selected the same numbers? What if he had to share his newly acquired wealth with three, four or even more lucky winners? Unfortunately that news was tantalizingly missing from the report. It was then that his thoughts were drawn to the little shop where he had purchased the newspaper. What if the phenomena were not a one off situation? If he were to return today would he be able to purchase tomorrow's paper? All thoughts of his postal round were forgotten as he ran from the house with only one thought in his mind; to return as quickly as possible to Guievere Alley……
Once more the doorbell jingled as he entered the little shop and was filled with excitement to see that all the newspapers carried the following days date. He threw a handful of coins on the counter, picked up a newspaper and hurried from the shop. As he turned into the High Street his curiosity overcame him and he stopped to read the headlines. The blood froze in his veins as they

proclaimed, *' LOCAL LOTTO WINNER IN FATAL ACCIDENT. READ FULL REPORT ON PAGE 3.'* With trembling hands he attempted to turn the page to find out where this 'fatal accident' would occur, determined to keep well away from wherever it was and so cheat fate. However, fate was in no mood to be cheated and as he struggled to turn the page, the skittish breeze that had appeared from nowhere had torn it from his grasp and sent it across the pavement and into the busy main road.

Nathaniel, with no thought for his own safety, chased after the elusive page and probably never felt a thing as the double deck bus mowed him down. The paramedics realized there was little they could do except remove the bloodstained newspaper, open at page 3 which announced that;

'A local man was killed in a road traffic accident on the High Street yesterday whilst attempting to retrieve a newspaper. In his possession was a jackpot winning lottery ticket worth over £6 million pounds. Camelot announced earlier today that the proceeds would be paid out to his estranged wife.'

Who could fail to be thrilled by the magnificent sight of an old fashioned locomotive, standing proudly on platform 1 and getting up a head of steam before chugging of to some far flung destination? Well Lionel Montague Smith for one. And why should any young man, who was as normal (I think) as any other red-blooded member of his gender, hold such unusual views? The answer of course can be found within the pages of this rather sad little tale entitled

A Different Train of Thought

Lionel Montague Smith did not like railways! In fact he positively hated them.
I suppose it all began when his parents, both keen railway buffs, decided to encumber their son with a name that was acronymic of the old London Midland & Scottish railway company. It didn't help that the main London to Glasgow line ran within spitting distance of Lionel's bedroom and the incessant daily (and nightly) traffic was, he decided early in his life, an infuriating experience that he could definitely live without. In fact it would be safe to surmise that Lionel had little love for railways or indeed anything that moved on them.

It therefore came as no surprise to him, when as a dissolute youth on holiday with his parents in the Caribbean; he visited a so-called voodoo fortune-teller, who along with many other strange predictions uttered the only one that really registered with Lionel.
"Beware o' the train man! That train is shor gonna get you 'less yo take good care yosself! Keep well away from de train 'cause it will sweep yo of your feet and yo gonna meet yo maker long afore yo time!"

Now such a prediction would cause most impressionable teenagers to ponder their immediate fate, but to one with an already inherent hatred of the permanent way, this latest pronouncement was tantamount to inducing positive paranoia in his breast. From that day forth he vowed that he would never travel on a train; would never set foot in a railway station and would avert his eyes if ever one came within his vision. Lionel became so obsessed with the fear that he even planned all his road journeys by such a route that he would never have to pass a railway station, travel within 100 metres of a mail line route or over have the need to negotiate a level crossing.

All went well for a number of years and so meticulous was his planning that to date he had never encountered a locomotive; seen even one puff of steam or heard one toot of a train whistle. However, all was to change on that fateful day in December as he drove to work along the tried and tested route he'd travelled many times before. As often happened during the rush hour, Lionel found himself in a traffic jam. The traffic in the outer lane was inching along while he was completely stationary. Still it was just another problem to be endured by the modern motorist, he mused stoically to himself as he glanced idly into his wing mirror.

The blood froze in his veins as he caught sight of the huge locomotive being transported on a low-loader. This is it, he reflected as the great black leviathan drew level with his car. He had a nightmare vision of the thick retaining chains snapping, allowing the inert beast to topple from its slowly moving platform and then squashing him and his little red mini very, very flat – The awful prophecy uttered all those years ago coming painfully true!

In a blind panic he put the car in gear, pressed hard on the accelerator; wrenched the steering wheel over and mounted the pavement. Startled pedestrians jumped out of his way as he battled to escape the scene of what he fervently convinced himself was his impending doom. He managed – Lord knows how – to travel about 50 metres or so before his journey was cut painfully short as he hit the unyielding concrete streetlamp and was hurled through the shattered windscreen. Just before he passed out, he was mightily relieved to see the still secured train pass him by without further incident.

Lionel, with his head incessantly and painfully thumping, slowly regained consciousness in the back of the ambulance that was taking him to the local hospital.
"How are you old chap," enquired the paramedic anxiously as he applied a dressing to a rather nasty gash on Lionel's forehead. "You took a nasty bump back there, but not to worry, we'll soon have you at A & E when this flipping barrier goes up."
"What barrier," responded Lionel apprehensively?
"Now don't worry son, once were over the level crossing we'll soon --------------." The paramedic froze in mid sentence as his recently comatose patient jumped from the stretcher; wrenched open the ambulance doors and leapt out into the road as if all the hounds of hell were pursuing him. In his panic and confused state of mind, instead of fleeing away from the source of his terror, he scaled the crossing gates and ran straight onto the railway lines just as the 8-25 express from Edinburgh to London came 'whooshing' by.

The paramedics and other startled onlookers let out a collective gasp as the iron monster sped past to reveal ---------- a very frightened and distressed Lionel cowering by the opposite barrier and calling loudly for his mum. How the train had missed him was a mystery to all who viewed the chaotic scene. The paramedics hurried over, wrapped him in a large red blanket and led him back to the waiting ambulance. Twenty minutes later, he was safely within the confines of St Margaret's General.

His recovery proved to be long and painful and but for the ministrations of Nurse Georgina Wilhelmina Riley, his stay in hospital would have been pretty unbearable. As the wearisome days passed slowly by, what started as a mere friendship gradually blossomed into a full-blown romance. By the time that Lionel was ready for discharge, the pair had grown so close that it was a surprise to no one that he had already 'popped the question' and had been accepted with what some may have construed as unseemly alacrity.

Their wedding plans progressed as well as any impending nuptials could, and it was with some relief to Georgina that on a somewhat blustery day in early October, they both stood at the altar, solemnly made their vows and eventually exchanged rings. Lionel had never really divulged his inordinate horror of railways to Georgina as he was determined to put the totally irrational fears behind him. Unfortunately the panic that had lain dormant in his breast during the past romantically focused weeks quickly rose to the surface as he gazed in awakening horror at the inscription thoughtfully added by his wife-to-be on the inner side of his golden band;

'LMS & GWR - United Forever'.

His immediate reaction was to flee the scene. He had been mad not to realize that his intended had initials that were also acronymic of yet another railway company, namely – Great Western Rail. The sight of the two initials intertwined on the ring had awoken his latent fears and that awesome prophecy made so long ago suddenly took on a new significance within his disturbed mind. Georgina, a true professional, sensed the impending panic attack and using all her skills as a trained nurse, managed to calm Lionel down to such a degree that the minister was able to continue with the service and much to Georgina's relief they did became Husband and Wife.

The happy couple stood at the top of the steep stone steps, happily posing for the many cameras that were recording the blessed event, as the now mischievous wind tugged playfully at Georgina's magnificent dress. All Lionel's earlier fears seemed to melt away, to be dispersed by the restless breeze.

"Just come forward a bit," shouted one of the many amateur photographers. Always one to please, Lionel obediently took a step forward just as the troublesome wind gusted and wrapped part of his new wife's trousseau around his ankles. His impetus carried him over the top step and unable to halt his forward momentum, he was sent crashing down the steep stony stairway, where he lay in a still huddled heap at the bottom -------------.

The stunned assembly let out a loud collective gasp as they stared at the inert form that only minutes earlier had uttered the fateful words 'I Do'. In the great scheme of things it was also somewhat ironic that the first people to rush to his aid happened to be a former engine driver and a signal box operative who both happened to have acquired First-Aid training in their previous occupations. Unfortunately and despite their combined efforts to resuscitate him, it soon became apparent to the assembled congregation and most poignantly his newly created widow that Lionel had indeed stumbled rather than 'shuffled off this mortal coil.'

The Coroner had pronounced that his skull had possibly fractured on his first contact with the hard unyielding step, but that the cause of death was undoubtedly the broken neck, sustained about halfway down the stony flight. However, the more upmarket tabloids managed to hit on to the true cause of Lionel's demise as the headlines screamed out the following morning: -

SIDERODROMOPHOBIC GROOM

MEETS HIS DOOM DUE TO

WAYWARD TRAIN!

Survivors!

She crouched low; her cowed young son by her side, pressing so hard against her breast that the frantic pounding of her terrified heart only added to his growing fears. He knew instinctively that now was not a good time to convey this fear by crying out. Absolute silence was essential. He knew from past experience that the smallest utterance would provoke unconstrained anger from his now slumbering father. A lazy, good-for-nothing patriarch who cared little for providing food or shelter or protecting his partner and their offspring from an intimidating environment that was little more than a jungle with danger lurking round every dark corner. He was selfish to the core and had no sense of family values or responsibilities and spent his seemingly pointless life in an endless round of gluttony, debauchery and noisy slumber.

That was of course when he was not ‘hanging out’ with his equally boorish and obnoxious mates at the local ‘watering hole’. Such visits did little to appease his naturally aggressive personality and he nearly always returned from such trips in a foul mood, often bearing the scars of an ill-tempered fracas with one or more of his so-called pals or rival gangs of thugs, keen to assert their authority on a rival’s patch. Like all bullies, he would stride belligerently in to the rude and quite basic living quarters; his thick mane of unkempt and unwashed hair standing on end as he roared menacingly his orders to be fed and woe betide his browbeaten partner if food was not instantly set before him.

And then of course there was his blatant infidelity. At first it had been just the odd occasion when he had returned home at all hours; reeking of the scent of some wanton female he had come across. She realized that she should have taken matters in hand at this early stage; yet ever optimistic she had hoped that the philandering would cease as he grew older and more mature and certainly with the arrival of the young ones. Unfortunately these happy occurrences seemed to promote the opposite effect, as if he sensed that his offspring were potential rivals to his impoverished kingdom and it was not unusual for him to be absent himself from home for days on end, with never an excuse or apology to offer when he decided to return.

And then again, what chance had he or any of his extended family really had all through their harsh existence? The neighbourhood had changed little over the years. It was a tough and unrelenting fight for survival, even for the bravest of residents; and as for the smaller and weaker occupants of this mean quarter, they were little more than punch bags for the thugs that relentlessly patrolled what was little more than a jungle – an absolute den of depravity, dissoluteness and iniquity. From an early age her mate had been subjected to the same harsh treatment that he was now handing out with impunity to his own son and heir. His mother too had felt the wrath of an impatient partner when things didn't go the way he expected them too. Yet despite all the abuse that she had endured over the years, she had raised up a large family of sons and daughters, which were undoubtedly her pride - and joy – And her reward? Desertion soon after they had learned to fend for themselves. It was therefore no surprise that her partner had turned out the way he had; a wretched bully with no thought for anyone or anything apart from his own selfish requirements.

So why would anyone choose to continue to live with such a lout? It was of course the old time worn story. Despite your resolve, you cannot choose whom you fall in love with and when the handsome guy who initially courted you with such care and attention turns out to be just another depraved Lothario when commitments have been made and children arrive – Well! What can you do? You just have to accept your lot and get on with life as best you can. It was true he would never be a family provider in the fullest sense of the word, other than in the fact that he did kept most forms of danger from the door. There were plenty of other unscrupulous thugs in the neighbourhood, who would think nothing of taking advantage of a lone female and her offspring, but thanks to papa and his love of a good scrap, they were relatively safe from such unwelcome attentions. Such was his prowess in these often-bloody encounters that he was grudgingly hailed by his fellows as the 'King' of the region.

Her thoughts returned to her present unhappy situation. The day had been neither good nor productive. She had fought off the unwelcome attentions of one she had considered a good pal of her partners, but like the rest of them it was obvious he could not resist the thrill of pursuing an unaccompanied female regardless of the consequences. The pitiful larder was empty. She had been unable to replenish their dwindling food stock due to matronly concern for her youngest son, who on the previous eve' had received yet another telling cuff from dad that had left him with a bruised and bloodied head. It had not been the first time that this insufferable father figure had violated her progeny and it was no surprise that as soon as they had been old enough to fend for themselves, her previous brood had left the family home to start a life of their own, far from the influence of the brute that passed as their father.

As for her inability to restock the larder - Well she was streetwise enough to realize that this had not been a prudent decision – not if she valued her wellbeing that is. As she knew from past and painful experience her partner was quick to anger on the slightest of pretexts, but where his belly was concerned, any reason for it not to be filled turned him into a virtual raging psychopath. However, despite her fears of the uncontrolled anger that would undoubtedly ensue due to the lack of consumable supplies, maternal concerns had taken precedence over survival instincts and this had prompted her to nurse her battered offspring rather than pursue provisions. This perhaps ill-judged assessment was the reason that mother and son were now in such a perilous situation, hardly daring to breathe for fear of invoking the wrath of the family head.

At that moment, although appearing to be slumbering, the insensitive brute raised his head as he detected a third party that now entered his living space. His terrified partner raised her head in order to ascertain the brave soul who had the temerity to approach her bestial partner. She choked down a strangled cry as she realized it was her sister, who knowing of her sibling's problems had rescued the day by bringing him some leftovers from her own meagre table. He eyed her and her timely offering and with little more than a growl for thanks, he hungrily devoured the lot.

A stab of pain lanced through the youngster's head, a reminder of the blow he had suffered the previous day, and he let out a low but discernable cry. Fortunately, his father, now satiated by the unexpected repast, was adopting a more languid attitude to his immediate family and mother and son knew instinctively that it was now safe to approach him. As mum tentatively revealed her presence, the seeming indifference of her partner was enough to inform her that she was forgiven – at least for the moment.

Mother and son, slowly and with great caution, approached the fearsome patriarch. Mum sat close by him and was rewarded by a gentle nuzzle in the region of her neck. Her offspring, still mindful of his recent beating, maintained a respectful distance from the now amorous couple, knowing that although her heart was not really in her show of feigned affection, it was an intuitive act she believed necessary to hopefully maintain some vestige of family harmony.

With his animal ardour now replete, he roughly pushed his partner away and cast a baleful eye in the direction of his son. What did he perceive? Some sort of threat to his authority? Surely not in one so young and helpless. But old habits die hard as he let out such a fearsome cry that the youngster fled towards the comparative safety of mum who stood her ground until the unfounded anger was subdued – at least for the moment. Both mother and son knew that the reprieve was only temporary and that tomorrow would bring again all the usual fear and tension. You see you didn't live in this violent neighbourhood, you existed – and if you were lucky you survived – Yes! Life was tough for a lioness and her cub in the heart of the Masai Mara.

WAR GAMES

The energy bolt zapped by so close to his cheek that he felt the searing heat from the thin but deadly ray as it vaporized the remains of the shattered window frame except for a few charred wooden splinters that were sprayed into Tommy's battle-hardened face. He peered out through the smoke laden atmosphere on to the carnage that surrounded him. Most of the buildings that were still standing were in ruins, torn apart by the incessant bombardment from the enemy's far superior weaponry.

He peered more in hope than expectation to see if any of his brave comrades had escaped the barrage that had rained down on this last outpost of human civilization and saw – nothing! Nothing that is except for the mutilated and lifeless bodies of probably the last Homo sapiens on planet Earth.
How had it come to this? The whole of mankind virtually wiped out by the superior firepower of an alien race that had appeared so friendly when their spacecraft had landed less than twelve months earlier. It was clear from the outset that the Martians were literally light years ahead of us in all departments and despite the fears of many. the conquest of Earth was certainly not in their itinerary. They had come in peace and appeared more than willing to share their superior knowledge with us.

Within months of their arrival, all illness and disease had been eradicated. They acknowledged that our civilization, despite many of its edicts being somewhat flawed, was heading in the right direction and by introducing just a few minor tweaks to the various constitutions had opened our eyes to a way of life that apparently suited all the many races and religions that made up the human race.

However, it is an unfortunate aspect of the human physiology, particularly prevalent in those that rule us, to believe that nobody does anything for nothing and as the

benign aliens, having turned the Sahara Desert into the new bread basket of Africa, began erecting a few modest buildings to house the power source that kept the area fertile, it was viewed by world leaders as the first steps towards planetary domination.
Crass stupidity is often accompanied by great cunning and those leaders who perceived the Martian activities as a threat to world peace believed that the only chance of success in any armed confrontation would only be achieved through the element of surprise – hence the sudden nuclear attack on their fleet of spacecraft.

At first it appeared that the cowardly plot had been successful and though the atomic weapons had hardly scratched the vessels, they all speedily departed, or so we thought, back to their home planet – how wrong can you be? Within hours tracking stations around the globe reported once more the presence of alien spacecraft, which were now heading to every inhabited area of the Earth. At some prearranged signal, each of what were now all to obviously well armed battleships commenced to unleash the terrible force of their weaponry. For the next few weeks death and destruction in the form of death rays and energy bolts rained down on every city, town and village on the planet. The people of earth were helpless in the face of such technologically superior weapons and despite the launching of countless atomic missiles at this marauding alien force; they didn't even scorch the paintwork of the death-dealing vessels.

A few hardy souls such as Tommy and some of his soldier buddies managed to regroup for a while in underground bunkers, which were a remnant of the old atomic shelters built in the 'cold war' era of nearly two centuries before. A search of these bunkers had revealed a small laboratory in which were discovered a number of sealed glass containers, each one labelled with the names of some of the deadliest bacterium and viruses known to man. They learned from one of their fellow evacuees, who apparently had worked in the field of virology, that in the event of open hostilities and as a last resort these containers would be packed into controlled missiles and delivered into the midst of the enemy ranks. Bacterial warfare it had been called but thankfully it had never been deployed in anger.

"If only we could get those darned Martians out of their spaceships," said Major Steel, the leader of the little group, "Maybe a few of these bottles tossed in their general direction could inflict more damage than our pesky guns and bombs......." Now maybe or maybe not you believe in the power of providence, but it so transpired that the all conquering Martians, realizing that although there was not a single being alive on the surface of Earth, their instruments indicated that that were still significant numbers skulking underground – And it was time for a bit of military sport.....

The first scout pods from the mother ship landed within a mile of the main bunker in which Tommy and his comrades-in arms were gazing unbelievably at the sight of their nine-foot tall, three-legged green-hued assailants disembarking awkwardly from their craft. They needed no space suits or breathing apparatus as their advanced medical technology apparently allowed them to live and breathe in the most hostile of environments – or so they thought. Tommy had bravely volunteered to go 'up top' armed with nothing more than a mortar launcher and a couple of dozen or so phials of the more deadly viruses such as ebola fever, anthrax and bubonic plague.

The Martians paused, more in amusement than fear, when they saw Tommy setting up his pathetic array of arms, and strange sounds that you could only imagine was the equivalent of Martian laughter erupted when the glass bottles burst in their midst. However, they became more agitated and hostile as the bombardment continued relentlessly and they began to advance towards the shattered ruin of what had once been a rather grand house in which Tommy, his ammunition spent, now sought refuge.

It soon became apparent that the viruses had been biologically enhanced and transmuted to become fast acting. Within minutes the initial brisk advance toward Tommy's bolthole began to slow significantly. The bright green iridescent colour of their skin grew pale and large red blotches began to erupt all over their extraterrestrial bodies. A number of the less disciplined aliens halted their advance and in a state of extreme agitation and fear returned to their ships; their aim obviously to seek help from this terrifying catastrophe that was engulfing them.

Technologically advanced they might be, clever they certainly were but this was probably the worst decision those Martians had ever made. The infected ones quickly passed on their deadly affliction to the rest of the invasion force and if anyone other than Tommy had been on the surface they would have been exhilarated to see the individual ships of this vast armada plunging to earth, one by one as the deadly viruses did their work.

However, Tommy had never felt more helpless as from his vantage point in the upper storey of the ruined house he saw the more determined of the Martians approach the airlock that was the entrance to the vast labyrinth of underground bunkers. With consummate ease they vaporized the ten-inch thick steel doors and let loose a cannonade of robotic controlled explosives. Two minutes later a terrific explosion announced that the bombs had done there worse and with a sickening realization Tommy was acutely aware that after millions of years of evolution, he was now probably the last human alive on the stricken planet. It was of little consolation when he observed the last of the aliens succumbing to the deadly viral attack so recently launched by Tommy. Not only was he now the last earthling alive but also the last intelligent creature capable of rational thought and reasoning to be drawing breath – His heart sank with the weight of such a realization.

It was in the depths of such abject despair that he heard the voice, very faint at first but gradually increasing in volume and insistence and there was no doubt that it was

human - and female. He realized with relief that he was not alone after all – The human race would continue to exist after all.
"Tommy" - He barely heard it at first. "Tommy" – He heard it a little clearer this time – "Tommy" – Yes, it was not his imagination; there was definitely someone there – "Tommy" – Now there was little doubt that someone else had survived the holocaust and the by high pitch of the voice there was no doubt that it was indeed female.
"Tommy" – The voice became more strident and persistent indicating a female of great strength and perseverance, and again he was convinced that despite all the trials and tribulations of recent months that perhaps there was hope for the world.
"TOMMY – I'm not going to shout again. Will you turn that flipping computer off and get down here – NOW! Your egg and chips are going cold!"

Ding-Dong Merrily On High

It was Christmas Eve; all appeared calm and peaceful as the first tumbling flakes of snow drifted lazily by the window set high up on the opposite wall to his bed. The Christmas tree in the corner of his room was resplendent with all manner of lights and baubles and all the walls were covered with Christmassy pictures, each one framed by bright bunches of holly, ivy and mistletoe. Yet despite this classic festive setting, the tree, the decorations or even the season itself held little joy or promise for Tom Scott, and as the evening newspaper plopped at the end of his bed he snatched impatiently at it and ignoring front page news that beer and petrol prices were falling, Deal Monster were offering a 2-course meal with wine for a 'fiver' at a local restaurant and that his local team were now heading the Championship league, he turned anxiously to the 'Births, Marriages & Death' section. It was to this last column that he now feverishly focused his attention.

There it was again! Just like the three previous evenings, sandwiched between 'Florence Emily Satterthwaite' and 'Francis George Smiley'. It jumped out of the page at him in bold, black 'Roman Face' -------

'Thomas Wilson Scott – Aged 68

Dearly beloved husband of Emily

Died 21st December 2012

"Sadly Missed"

Sadly missed! Was that the best epitaph she could come up with? That was the trouble with Emily – No flair; no style; no imagination. What was wrong with *'A lion among men'* or perhaps *'He will make heaven a happier place'* or even *'His bowling skills were legendary.'* - But what was he thinking? The whole scenario was crazy. 'Passed away quietly in his sleep' continued the bland eulogy.

"I'll say it was quiet," he muttered angrily to himself. "They didn't even bother to inform me!"

Tom Willy Scott was justifiably annoyed. Granted, he had for the past year or so experienced some minor internal problems that had culminated in his recent collapse, which he presumed was the reason he had been admitted to the clinic for treatment - but dead! That was, he considered indignantly, carrying things just a little to far.

He sincerely hoped that Emily would be visiting him later that evening. For all her many faults she had never suffered fools gladly and no doubt she'd soon have the mix-up sorted out with those 'idiots' who were running the paper. Mind you, since he'd been admitted she had not bothered to call on him at all – not once, although to be fair, hadn't she always confessed, with that little tremor of her bottom lip, that she never really had the 'stomach' for visiting such depressing institutions like hospitals.

However, three nights now! They'd never been parted for such a lengthy period during the whole of their married life, and while there was never a good time to be 'snatched' from the bosom of your family, Christmas just had to be the worst imaginable. Surely she would endeavour to put in an appearance this night of all nights?

His thoughts drifted back to that untimely announcement, and the more he considered the situation, the more convinced he became that the fates were transpiring against him. He recalled that after seeing the first notification in the paper, he had asked his personal ward orderly to call the classified section of the newspaper on his behalf, with specific instructions to cancel the current upsetting insertion and substitute in its place that famous quote by the immortal Mark Twain; *'The reports of my death have been greatly exaggerated.'*

It now appeared that either the orderly or the classified clerk at the newspaper offices had forgotten to process his revised instruction.

"Still," he chuckled to himself, "it will be good for a laugh." He couldn't wait to see the faces of his mates when he next walked into his local bowling club. The last his bowling chums had seen of him was when he had been carried semi-conscious from the green to the waiting ambulance muttering, "Please - Just one more end."

"Great Scott!" they would probably exclaim on seeing his return from the hospital. His smile broadened as the full significance of the pun struck him.

'Funny old place this clinic' he mused to himself. 'Wonder why they couldn't treat me at the local hospital? I guess they must have some special equipment for my particular condition – Whatever that may be. Why does it always seem to be that the last person to know of their prognosis is the patient themselves?' And then of course there was the location. Tom thought he knew his local area pretty well but could not recollect hearing of such a specialist clinic in the region. 'Must be one of them new private places that seem to be springing up all over,' he cogitated. He had a vague recollection of passing through a pair of large ornamental gates and seeing a large ornate letter H affixed over the top; obviously denoting a hospital of some kind. He also recalled the elderly porter or doorman, dressed in an all white uniform, taking an interminable time entering his admission details. In fact at one time it appeared they were going to turn him away, but eventually he was admitted.

'It really is as quiet as the grave this place - but actually quite pleasant and relaxing,' he further reflected. The only noises he had heard during his stay had been the faraway sound of a choir singing festive songs, accompanied by what appeared to be an orchestra of harps and trumpets and he had to admit that he had never heard anything quite as moving and pure before. He made a mental note to find out who they were as the experience had been truly heavenly. At the far end of his room was an arched window and he supposed that he must be on one of the higher floors, as all he could see were a succession of white fluffy clouds floating serenely by. The only other person he had seen during his brief sojourn apart from the white bearded 'Doctor', who, after Tom had been settled in, had poured long and hard over his admission details that had been entered by the elderly porter in a large leather-bound book; was the somewhat cherubic faced 'orderly', who flitted in and out of his private room at regular intervals, seemingly having no other duties but to care exclusively for Tom.

Still, he wasn't complaining. He had managed to get Tom the local newspaper each evening during his enforced stay and for that he was grateful. As he had often remarked to Emily on seeing the paper boy coming up the path of their little suburban bungalow;
'I think I'd pass away if I didn't get to read my evening paper.'

He wondered when they would actually start his treatment. To date he had not been overly concerned as he had appreciated the rest. He theorized that they were probably allowing him to stabilize, but then again – three days was rather a lengthy period to tie up precious bed-space. He promptly decided that he would ask the doctor to be a little more specific regarding his exact medical condition when he next saw him.

The more he thought about it, the more he convinced himself that perhaps there was nothing that seriously wrong with him. Certainly nothing life threatening that a good rest wouldn't cure. On further reflection, he couldn't recall one moment of pain since his admission to the clinic. Perhaps the original diagnosis had been hasty and that maybe they should reconsider the findings. Yes! He was now more determined than ever to seek, nay demand a second opinion before some overly eager surgeon started 'messing about' with his internal 'plumbing'.

As if on cue, the white-bearded 'doctor' strode purposefully into the little private room and began looking around in a state of great agitation.

"Doctor," began Tom somewhat timidly, "I'm not convinced that I should really be here! Is there any chance of me going home, at least over the Christmas period, while perhaps you re-think my condition?

"Oh no Thomas! There's no mistake. As sure as my name's Peter I can honestly say that I've never yet let anybody in who wasn't fully qualified to enter. Ah! There it is!" he remarked with relief at seeing the evening paper at the foot of the bed. “It’s the special Christmas edition full of all sorts of heavenly articles. I do hope its not crumpled before ‘G’ sees it. Can’t be doing with a messy paper can’t ‘G’. Shouts fit to raise the devil he does and that would never do – not in here. Oh! By the way your permanent residency order has received the seal of approval and I’ve signed your chit for a novice halo and beginner’s harp and later we can get you measured for your scarlet and gold robes for the lad’s birthday bash tomorrow. You know Tom, you’re going to make just about the most perfect Christmas angel!!!”

AWAY IN A - BUS SHELTER?

"Oh my God, I don't believe it," bellowed Joe as he opened the official looking brown envelope that along with his overdraft statement, final demands for credit card debts and unpaid utility bills was the extent of the mail delivered that morning to the small but neat terraced house in downtown Nuneaton.

"What's up now?" responded Mavis, his long-suffering spouse from the kitchen as she silently cursed the ancient and temperamental toaster.

"It's only the blasted Tax Office again about last year's underpayment of VAT and income tax. If I've told them once I've told 'em a thousand times, I need more time to sort it all out - But they're not having any."
"What are they saying now?" she replied despondently as she finally got to spread the last of the marmalade on their half-done breakfast toast.
"They're telling us we have to go to the head office in Bermondsey of all places, and in the depth of winter as well - it's just not on."
"What! Both of us - Don't they realize we live in Nuneaton and that I'm nearly nine months pregnant?"
"Eey Mavis lass, do you think Tax Collectors are bothered about mere trivialities like that? They'd get you over from the other side of the world and drag you from your deathbed if they thought they could wring another penny or so out of you - They're heartless - that's what they are - blooming heartless." Joe replied grimly.
"Well I reckon you should ring and have another 'do' with 'em - and tell 'em you want to speak to the organ grinder this time not the monkey." She added sternly..........
An hour or so later, Joe slammed the phone back into its cradle in undisguised frustration and announced angrily, "Knew it would be a waste of bloody time. We have to go and that's the end of it - There's just no reasoning with 'em."
"Did you talk to the top man or did they fob you off - again?"
"No they didn't fob me off again. They put me through to a Mr Herod, top dog there I reckon, and a right officious blighter he was as well, spoke like he owned the place."

"And so!" replied Mavis impatiently, "What was the outcome?"
"I bet that guy frightens babies," proclaimed Joe furiously. "I'm sorry love but there's no getting out of it I'm afraid. We both have to go. I only hope that temperamental old Datsun of ours can get us there in one piece without breaking down."
"Can't understand why they want to see both of us though; you're the head of the family joinery business after all."
"That's as may be pet but remember I had to put your name on the agreement as a guarantor for any debts that the business might incur and that's why they want to see you as well."
"Don't you 'pet' me; JOE'S JOLLY JOINERS, I told you it was a daft name; it's no wonder you hardly get any orders - and another thing......." Joe held up his hand to cut off his wife in mid sentence.
"Look! It's no good us falling out about it - again. Let's just get ourselves to Bermondsey and sort this flaming mess out once and for all........"

The old Datsun made heavy weather of the long drive but eventually a snow-covered road sign informed them that they were '***Now entering the Borough of Bermondsey - Please drive carefully.***' The journey had taken much longer than they had allowed for and as the garish streetlights flickered on they realized that the tax office would be well and truly closed for business. There was little they could do now but find a cheap hotel or guesthouse for the night.

"Another one full up," announced Joe crossly as he trudged back to the car. "It seems that there's a top artist performing in the local theatre tonight and there's not a room to be had anywhere in the town," he added.
"Charming!" moaned a now disconsolate Mavis. "So what's the grand plan ***nowwww!"*** Mavis clutched at her stomach in agonizing pain as the first contraction caught her completely unawares.
"I just knew this would happen," moaned Mavis through gritted teeth. "Well Mr Clever Clogs joiner, just what do you propose to do now?" she added as her waters broke, making a complete mess of the little car.
"We'll get you out of there for a start," replied Joe calmly. "Look! There's a bus shelter over the road. Let's get you inside while I ring for an ambulance," he added reassuringly. Joe helped his wife over to the rather grubby shelter that smelled strongly with a combination of sweat, fish & chips and stale cigarette smoke. There was a grubby wooden bench in the far corner of the shelter to where Joe guided his somewhat distressed spouse.
"Tell them to hurry; the contractions are getting closer," Mavis whined, gripping his hand tightly.
Tem minutes passed, which seemed like an eternity to the frantic couple - And then a bright light shone above them.
"What we got 'ere then?" spoke a rather strident voice as the owner shone his torch at the pitiful duo on the bench.
"Who are you?" barked Joe defensively, thinking perhaps they were about to be mugged.
"Calm down laddie; I'm PC Shepherd and this 'ere is my assistant PCSO Lamb. We've come to tell you that the ambulance has got stuck in traffic due to this show that's

on in town tonight. Meanwhile we've been directed 'ere from on high to keep an eye on you both till it arrives. Stop nosey folk from flocking round yer and the like......"
The words were hardly out of his mouth when with a screech of brakes, a large white van came to a halt at the entrance. At first Joe thought it was the ambulance - But no such luck. The large red writing on the side of the van proclaimed that it belonged to

'Wiseman & Sons - Gifts For All Ages.'

Moments later, three rather anxious looking men entered the grubby shelter.
"Thank the Lord," said the elder of the trio with a sigh of relief - "See you two doubters, I said it was a police car parked outside. Now perhaps the two 'bobbies' 'ere can direct us to the theatre before we miss the show completely."
"If it weren't for that dodgy Sat-Nav of yours Uncle Goldie we would have been at the right place ages ago," retorted his nephew Frankie.
"Fancy anyone buying a GPS called 'Bright Star'" added Frankie's younger brother Merv', "Call yourself wise? I think we'd have got from East Grinstead quicker if we'd followed an actual star rather than that useless piece of electronic rubbish."
Before anyone could add further comment, two more people entered the now rather congested shelter, introducing themselves as Gabriel and Angela and declaring that they were 'Street Pastors' or as they were more commonly called by the good people of

Bermondsey, 'Angels of the Night' and that their duties were to help people in distress.
"Well you've come to the right place tonight Gabe' and Ange', there's no one more distressed than me at the moment." Mavis moaned from her prone position on the hard and very uncomfortable bench.
"Don't worry ma'am, we're both trained in midwifery skills and if the worst comes to the worst then we can assist at the birth.
Once again the grimy and smelly shelter was bathed in light from above. This time it was from a Police helicopter, hovering above the somewhat ramshackle building to inform them by loud hailer that the road had now been cleared and that the ambulance was on its way. It continued to hang there in the night sky like a flaming star, offering guidance for all who wished to follow its beckoning light. Moments later the impending arrival of the ambulance was confirmed as, from the far distance, the assembly heard the reassuring wail of a siren - However, Mavis feared it would not arrive on time. With a wail that would have done justice to a demented banshee, she clutched frantically at Joe's arm before declaring to all and sundry -
"It's coming!"

Gabe' and Ang' did what they were trained to do and seconds later the silence that had now descended on the shelter was broken by the cry of a newborn child. The assembled humans let out a collective sigh of relief and clapped and cheered at the safe arrival of the newcomer. From the rafters above was heard a fluttering of many wings as the previously disturbed pigeons finally settled and cooed their own non-human greetings. The soft squeak of a somewhat bedraggled mouse and the gentle mewling of a rather mangy alley cat accompanied this salutation as in perfect peace and understanding all the shelter's occupants paid homage to the child.

It was then that Joe emerged from the group and held aloft the tiny bundle of humanity who had arrived in such dire but nevertheless welcoming circumstances and announced to the world with fatherly pride, joy and exultation,

"It's a girl! - We're going to call her Jessica!"

The Ghost of a Chance

Do I believe in ghosts? Well, if you had asked me last year at this time I would have probably replied in the negative. However much has happened in the past twelve months to convince me that not only do they exist but that they also possess a cunning and quite fiendish sense of retribution. My days as a fraudster were well behind me after nearly getting sussed when I conned a rich old geezer called Sir Henry something-or-other, who lived in some posh 'gaff' in Mayfair. Nearly three quarters of a million I cleared on that particular Ponzi scheme. Apparently the shock saw the old geezer off and - But wait! I'm getting a little ahead of myself. Let me take you back to the day when I first met – or rather heard my particular ghost.........

I had taken the rather short step from conman to gambler and was having my usual run of luck – all bad - at the Blackjack table when with my last chips committed I was dealt a ten and a six. I placed my palms together as if in supplication; the dealer was smirking as if he knew I was destined to walk home that night and the player to my left drummed his fingers impatiently on the baize covered table as he waited for my decision. I was on the verge of calling 'stick' when a voice in my ear whispered, quite audibly, *'Twist'*. Like a fool I repeated the foolish advice and before I could correct myself the jubilant dealer dealt me - the two of clubs. This of course meant that I now held 18, not the best score in the world but then again it sure beat the 16 that I held a moment ago. Yes – I figured that 18 had at least a fighting chance of beating a dealer that had relentlessly turned over a seemingly unending succession of 19's and 20's, interspaced with an uncanny number of 21's.

'Stick' was on the tip of my tongue when the same voice hissed in my ear *'Twist'*. Like a fool I concurred and asked the dealer for another card. I think he was more surprised than me when the card turned out to be another deuce – this time hearts. My heart raced. I was holding 20. Surely this was enough for me to recoup at least some of my losses? The dealer turned automatically to the 'finger drummer' convinced that only a blithering idiot would risk taking a further card. *'Twist'* came the strident voice once more, although it appeared that only I could hear it.

I fought hard against this seemingly preposterous advice and could hardly believe my own voice as it croaked the senseless command - 'Twist'. With a mocking gleam in his eye and a flourish that could only mean 'so' long sucker', he turned over – the ace of spades. They told me after that the odds for achieving a 'five card trick' with an initial hand of 16 were many thousands to one. But I – or rather the disembodied voice had actually done it. It was somewhat academic that the dealer held two kings, which beat everyone else at the table – I had won!
The next hour or so passed as if in a dream. Every hand I was dealt was a winner, thanks to my ghostly advisor and soon I was almost hidden behind the growing pile of chips that were now stacked high in front of me. There was no doubt that the 'House' was worried and in an attempt to stymie my run of 'luck' they decided to close the table and invited me to try my luck perhaps at the roulette wheel. Now every serious gambler knows that there is only one winner at this game and it's certainly not 'Johnny Punter'. It was then that I felt the tug at my sleeve and the word *'Come'* whispered in my ear. Again, as if under some strange spell I allowed the invisible hand to lead me to the roulette table. A house attendant followed carrying my chips, and politely informed me that they amounted to just short of £5,000. On hearing this, my first instinct was to cash them in and leave the casino for the first time ever in the 'black' – My unseen companion though had other plans for me that night.
'Evens' he announced with total conviction and I duly pushed all my chips towards the recommended slot. The little white ball flew around the periphery of the brightly

coloured wheel, holding the gaze of the attendant players as if in a trance before eventually loosing momentum as it clattered over the red and black numbers before eventually nestling in number 22 – EVENS!....... My head spun as I realized that I had doubled my money in the blink of an eye. Now! It really was time to go – My faceless companion had other ideas as once again he urged *'Evens'*. A minute later I was worth £20,000!
I pinched myself hard to ensure that this was not some fantastic dream and the ensuing pain convinced me that the events were indeed happening. I hoped that the voice would now be stilled, as surely this lucky streak could not continue. My hopes were dashed as the croupier removed the 'dolly' from the table and once again set the wheel in motion. *'32'* was the next ghostly command. I just couldn't do it. Only a fool would bet on a single number and only then with a nominal amount. Yet here was my 'friend' advising – nay – demanding that I gamble £20,000 on number 32. My thoughts were in utter turmoil as I then heard the croupier announce. 'No more bets please.' The moment had passed and I had defied the advice – or so I thought. As I gathered my senses it was in abject horror that I realized my complete stash was nestling on the table – next to – number 32.
The next minute was like an eternity as my eyes were transfixed on the spinning wheel, as was every eye in the casino that night. 'Clack-clickety-clack' sounded the little white ball as it bounced along the succession of numbers before finally settling in the little recess – with the number 32 above it! There was a collective gasp from a hundred throats as I made a quick mental calculation. The

croupier confirmed my answer - £700,000. He also announced that the table was now closed for the evening. What he really meant was that I had achieved what every gambler dreams of – I'd broken, or at least very badly dinted, the casino bank.

I was ushered swiftly into the manager's office where he politely inquired as to how I would like my winnings paid. A cheque? A banker's draft, or perhaps! – I rather rudely interrupted him at this juncture and told him of my distrust of the banking system and informed him that I would only accept my dues in hard cash. I thought that this may present a problem but without a flicker of emotion he produced a small travelling case from under his desk, opened the huge Chubb safe and with meticulous care filled it with the requisite amount of large denomination banknotes. The task completed, he advised me to take a taxi home as it would be foolhardy to walk the streets of the metropolis carrying such a huge amount of cash, a suggestion with which I readily concurred.

I settled into the rear seat of the taxi and was about to give the location of the somewhat seedy lodging house where I was staying when once again the voice, which by now was becoming all too familiar, whispered *'Mayfair Mansions'*. As in a dream I repeated the destination to the cabbie and with a 'Right you are guv' we set off. Ten minutes later the cab stopped outside the prestigious address as the voice once again instructed me to head for *'Apartment 4'*. I was somewhat surprised to find the substantial door ajar and with a hesitant step I entered the plush apartment

The only light came from the embers of a dying fire and yet I could see that someone was seated in the high wing-backed chair. As I approached, the chair swung slowly around to reveal the smiling shadowy figure of – the late Sir Henry What's-is-name! The smile slowly turned into a rictus grin, which in turn grew to fiendish laughter, so loud and terrifying that I dropped the case containing my 'winnings' and clapped my shaking hands to my ears in a frantic but unsuccessful attempt to block what had now become the apparent screaming of demented demons. I felt my legs buckle as the room swam into darkness and I slumped senseless to the floor.

When I finally recovered my numbed senses, it was to find the case lying open at my feet, divested now of banknotes but filled with an assortment of candlesticks, ornaments, clocks etc, what one could perhaps describe as a typical housebreaker's haul. Of Sir Henry, there was nary a sign and as a loud pounding began to shake the large front door followed by a strident command of 'POLICE! – OPEN UP', I noticed just one crumpled banknote on the wing-backed chair bearing the three chilling words –

'Evens, I believe!'

And The Poor Get ---- Monkeys?

Ah! Most esteemed traveller, welcome to my humble guesthouse and may I pour you a long cooling glass of sweet and refreshing mango juice before you dine on our simple but nourishing locally resourced and quite unique curry. What is that you say sir? You prefer a steak, medium rare? Ah! Sir, were that but possible then I would prepare it myself and season it with the finest herbs and spices that this land is famed for, but alas sir, this is the poorest of villages in an impoverished region. What is that you say sir? Why are we so destitute in a land famed for its bounteous and gastronomic delights? The question is well put and deserves an honest answer, which I shall attempt to expound on, but please, do not let the telling of this tale distract you from your meal. You must eat whilst I attempt to enlighten.

Honourable sir, your curiosity is undoubtedly roused and you may well ask why all the people in our humble village are so poor and downcast, yet I assure you that it was not always this way. Many moons ago we were a happy and thriving community, with each man working his little patch of land to provide for his family, with always a little surplus that was carried into town where it was sold to provide a few luxuries. We were not rich but we had all that was required to ensure contentment – that is until the fateful day when Siddi-Ben-Aheb arrived in our village.

Siddi-Ben-Aheb was an Arabian merchant who made a prosperous living by buying and selling all manner of goods, and by the jewelled rings on his fingers and the splendour of his flowing robes, he was obviously a master of his profession. That first night he had sat down with the headman and the elders of our little community and explained the reason for his visit. It appeared that the local chieftain, on a recent visit to a neighbouring tribe, had gazed with envy at the magnificent robes that had adorned his rival. He was informed that each garment was made from the skins of one hundred green monkeys and that all who set eyes on it admired greatly the unusual costume. So jealous was the chieftain of this wonderful robe that he summoned Siddi-Ben-Aheb to his court and commanded him to obtain all the green monkeys that he could in order that not only he but also all the ladies of the harem could bedeck themselves in such glorious attire.

Now it so happened that the forest that surrounded our humble settlement was teeming with green monkeys. The headman had winked knowingly at the wisest of the elders; a gesture that signified that there were many dinars to be made at the expense of Siddi-Ben-Aheb.
“And how much are you willing to pay for these green monkeys?” inquired the headman.
“Because of the royal decree I am instructed to pay 10 dinar for each live specimen.” There was the intake of many breaths as the assembly heard this figure as 10 dinars was more than a man could earn from a dozen visits to the marketplace.

And so it was that the following day that every able-bodied person in the village set aside their normal duties and went instead into the forest to catch green monkeys. Siddi-Ben-Aheb was as good as his word and after a week, a compound that had been constructed now contained well over 200 chattering green monkeys and each captor had duly received the agreed sum in shiny new coins. As you can imagine, there was much feasting and drinking among our people as a result of their newly acquired wealth. But sir, as I’m sure you are aware, when riches are obtained by very little effort, people become somewhat lazy and dissolute and despite the generous rewards, many of the previously diligent villagers tired of the monkey business (sic) as now the beasts were not as easy to locate and the hunters found themselves having to journey much deeper into the surrounding countryside in an effort to find them.

When this news was conveyed to Siddi-Ben-Aheb, being the astute businessman he was, and to stir the people from their torpor, he duly announced that from the morrow he would pay 30 dinars per monkey. Now this indeed was an incentive they could not be ignored and so with renewed vigour all the villagers scoured the land for miles around and before long there were another 100 or so monkeys captured and incarcerated. However, once again the villagers tired of their task and the once plentiful supply of green monkeys into the compound was reduced to a mere trickle.

It was at this juncture that Siddi-Ben-Aheb had called for a meeting of the whole village population. With much breast beating and hand wringing he informed the massed gathering that the chieftain had decreed that unless many more monkeys were made available – and soon - then Siddi-Ben-Aheb would find himself about a foot shorter – he would lose his beautifully tonsured head! The threat had certainly had the desired effect as through gritted teeth he informed the assemblage that he was now reluctantly prepared to pay 200 dinars for every green monkey captured. The collective gasp was awesome to behold. This offer was verily a king's ransom to the humble villagers.

A great safari was arranged to scour the countryside and every able-bodied man, woman and child was enlisted to the task. In the meantime Siddi-Ben-Aheb had informed the headman that he needed to make a three-day journey to the chieftain's palace in order to procure the extra money required to pay for the monkeys. Now it so happened that Siddi-Ben-Aheb had a manservant called Abdul, who he left in charge during his enforced absence. There was little love lost between master and servant and Siddi-Ben-Aheb was barely an hour departed when Abdul approached the headman with a most tempting proposition. He told of the cruel way he was treated by his master and in a move to get even he offered to sell all the monkeys in the cages to the villagers for 100 dinars each, which would save them the bother of an extended hunt and still leave them with a handsome profit when they then sold them back to Siddi-Ben-Aheb for 200 dinars each.

The villagers, in attempting to obtain the necessary cash to pay Abdul for the caged monkeys, spent the next day gathering up and selling all their worldly goods and possessions. The greedier ones had even visited bankers and moneylenders in the nearby town in order to raise enough cash to buy as many monkeys as possible. At last the prescribed amount was raised to buy every single monkey, which was duly handed over to Abdul in exchange for the key to the compound.

The following day was spent in high expectation as each man, woman and child mentally counted the riches that were soon to come their way. The elders had met in the ancient communal hut and were discussing how they would use the money to make life easier for the community. The headman proposed that an irrigation system be built so that water for the fields would no longer have to be brought by bucket. The medicine man pleaded that he badly needed a new pot in which to infuse the medicinal herbs for the sick. Just then a small beam fell with a clatter from the sagging roof, which prompted the whole gathering to decide that a new communal hut should be at the top of any wish list.

On the day after, hopes were still elevated as the villagers knew that Siddi-Ben-Aheb's journey was indeed a long one with many dangers to be faced, so for him to be a little late was not that surprising. On the third day there were signs of distress and consternation and this time it was we, the villagers who were hand wringing and breast-beating. By the end of the week the whole populace had been reduced to despondency and blind panic. As for Siddi-Ben-Aheb and Abdul they were never seen again. They now had all our money; the bankers and moneylenders had our promissory notes and we the naïve villagers ------ we had the most expensive monkeys in the whole of this fair land!

And now sir, I see your plate is virtually empty, which tells me that the humble dish was well received. What was that you said sir? The meat from which the curry was made was unknown to you but despite this unfamiliarity you say it was quite succulent and indeed most acceptable, You enquire if it were beef or chicken, but I must inform you neither was used in the preparation of the dish. We use instead that of which there is abundance, nay a surfeit in and around our humble village – Need I enlighten you further sir?

SEVENTH HEAVEN

Brian was an inveterate gambler. He would bet on anything where a result was possible. His consuming passion for trying to beat the odds had all started on his seventh birthday when his twin sister Bryony had bet him that she could open her presents faster than him and that the loser of the wager would then hand over their most cherished birthday gift. Unable to resist the challenge he had responded in a way that was to shape the rest of his life. The fact that he had actually won the bet only reinforced the feeling of total euphoria he experienced as he took possession of Bryony's 'Tiny Tears' doll. However, there was little reason for his sister to be fretful as with all fixated gamblers he could just not refuse a flutter and so within a week, not only had she won her dolly back by predicting which raindrop would reach the bottom of the window pane first but had also relieved him of his 'Action Man' by guessing how many sweets were in the bag of 'pick & mix' (of course she omitted to inform him that she had counted them first).

Over the years, his fervour for gambling had gained momentum and whilst he had experienced a certain amount of luck with the wagers he struck, most of it was of the 'hard' variety. His stake of ten week's pocket money that Preston North End would win the F.A. cup in 1964 or the week's paper delivery wages that he wagered on man setting foot on the moon in 1968 only served to fuel his fervour. It was of no great surprise to anybody then when he entered his adult years virtually penniless but retaining the gambler's unshakeable belief that one-day his luck would change and he would hit it big.

Now most gamblers are superstitious and place great faith in signs and omens. Brian was no exception to this notion, particularly when it involved his one overriding gambling infatuation – Horseracing. Most days would find him poring over the various racing journals before making his daily trip to the bookmakers to place his bets. Many times his predetermined selections had been influenced and amended by occurrences that happened during the journey to the betting shop. There was the time when a black cat had crossed his path and he realized that 'Puss-in-Boots' was running in the 3-30 at Chepstow (fell at the first fence) and just had to be backed. Unfortunately, as his knowledge of the French language was very limited, he had failed to notice that 'Chat Noir' was entered in the 2-30 at Aintree (won at 13 to 2), which he missed completely. However, such disappointments, and there were many, failed to dampen his firmly held convictions that signs, omens and portents should be followed.

It would have surprised no one then when he awoke on a particular sunny morning in early July after experiencing the most vivid dream about the number '7'. The day had dawned to find him trembling with excitement and anticipation, wondering just how to interpret the dream and turn it to his advantage. Completely oblivious to all irrelevant and insignificant daily functions such as ablutions and breakfasting, he turned feverishly instead to his beloved racing magazines and after a quick perusal was not at all surprised to learn that there was a horse running at Newbury that day called 'Lucky Seven' and quoted at very generous odds as well. Brian knew instantly that all the previous years of frustration, disappointments and near misses were behind him; this was to be the day when all his deepest desires and fondest dreams were destined to come true and he just sensed that before the day was out he would be a wealthy man.

Brian had little spare cash to lay his hands on but through various means, some not entirely honest, he had managed to scrape together the rather prophetic sum of £7,000. So excited had he become at the thought of becoming rich and as Newbury racecourse was only 7 miles and a short bus ride away, he decided he would attend the meeting in person and be there at the winning

post when 'Lucky Seven' swept past, way out in front of the rest of the field.
As he boarded the bus he noticed that it was the No 7 to Newbury, a town that just happened to have 7 letters in its name. He glanced at his ticket and found that he had been allocated – yes, you've guessed – seat No 7. During the short ride to the racecourse he further perused his paper and learned that his horse was entered in a novices chase of 7 furlongs and would not only be displaying the number 7 but had also been drawn at No 7 and would be carrying a 7stone-7lb apprentice jockey who was running in only his seventh race. Suffice it to say but the race was also the seventh on the card on this most significant of days, July 7th – All the signs were there – It was all stacking up very nicely; very nicely indeed....
As he passed through gate No 7 of the paddock area his ingrained gambler's reasoning kicked in. He knew that if he placed the full £7,000 wager with one bookie then this would surely drive down the starting price of the horse. He decided he would spread his bets across a number of the very obliging gentlemen under the large umbrellas who had relieved him of so much cash over the years - But just how many should he visit? And then the answer was before him in a flash – Why seven of course.
He tingled with excitement and expectation when the final bet was placed with no unexpected incidents and he knew he must have a stiff drink to settle his nerves. At the crowded bar he ordered a large whiskey and lemonade and was visibly shaking with disbelief when the aforementioned mixer turned out to be 7-up – It was like taking candy from the proverbial baby.

There was still time to kill before the race was due to start. Brian took his drink and went into the lounge to watch the latest cricket commentary on TV. It was the opening day of the 3rd test against Australia and England certainly had the upper hand. They had bowled the Aussies out for 177, with their new all-rounder hero having taken 7 for 77. The same player was now at the wicket with his score on 70. Brian watched with mounting tension as the player clipped an over pitched delivery into the outfield. They ran 2 and turned for a third that was risky. The fielder retrieved the ball and shied at the stumps. It missed by a whisker and he watched in awe as it eluded all the fielders and raced to the boundary – scoring an improbable 7 runs and moving the player in question up to 77 – Brian stood up as if in a trance and walked to the bar for another drink....

At last the 7th race was announced and Brian hurried to the parade ring to catch a glimpse of the animal that was going to make him a very rich man. 'Lucky Seven' was splendidly turned out and put the rest of the horses in the ring to shame. The jockey's silks were intriguing but I shall not bore you with the number of green stripes on the shirt or the number of yellow dots on the cap. Suffice it to say they matched well with the theme of the day. The jockeys climbed aboard their horses and after receiving last minute instructions from owners and trainers were led down to the starting gate. A buzz of excitement and anticipation rose to a crescendo from the throats of the eager race goers as the starter's flag descended, heralding the hoarse (sic) call that followed such a prelude – 'There off.'

A short time later, just over 7 minutes or so to be precise, Brian could be found sitting once more in the bar, his tear-stained face looking the absolute picture of disbelief. His sobs attracted the attention of a number of sympathetic punters with one caring soul placing a comforting arm around his now hunched shoulders.
"Don't take it so hard old son, you can't win 'em all. Where did your horse finish then?
"Seventh" came the mournful cry!
Now let this be a salutary lesson to all you would be punters who set store by portents and omens – Read them carefully before making your decision. If Brian had possessed just a smidgen more of the French language and if he had delved a little deeper into his racing chronicles he would have learned that at the Aintree evening meeting that very day in the 7 O'clock race, there was a horse running called Soixante-Dix-Sept. It had romped home at the generous odds of 7 to 1 – C'est la vie!

A NEAR CATASTROPHE

Tom clung in terror to his perilous perch high above the snowy terrain below. All four limbs were paralysed by a combination of abject fear and fatigue. The harder he tried to free himself from his unfortunate predicament the less responsive his once highly toned body became.

Tom had been an enthusiastic climber all his life and to date he had met every dizzy challenge with seemingly effortless ease and assurance. Mountains, rock- faces, buildings, in fact virtually anything that presented a climbing challenge, whether it be a natural feature or a man-made structure, Tom appeared to be hard-wired to such a degree that he just had to scale it. It was obvious to his peers that the old adage of 'Why do you want to climb it?' would have received the obvious hackneyed response – 'Because it's there'.

Like many of his breed, Tom preferred to climb alone. He gained great satisfaction from knowing that all that he had accomplished had been through his own efforts and endeavours, with help from no one. However, as he now clung desperately to the precarious perch on which he found himself, his last vestiges of strength and stamina been sucked from his slim frame by the biting wind that had come sweeping in from the East, carrying with it the threat of even more snow, memories of more glorious accomplishments flashed through his mind.

It seemed as though it was only yesterday that he had clambered almost nonchalantly up the side of a recently erected 30-storey office block that had been considered 'unassailable' by the young architect who had designed it, knowing only to well the challenge that such a structure would offer the growing number of free runners and urban mountaineers in the country who, like Tom, viewed any such building as a test of their prowess.

In his mind he could still hear the 'Oohs' and 'Aahs' of the assembled crowd below as they followed his steady progress up what appeared to be a smooth vertical wall of concrete, little realizing that Tom had the uncanny knack of finding a hold where others would undoubtedly fail. The cheer that rang out as the climber in the black coat sprang onto the flat roof could only be matched by the cries of anguish and despair issuing from a certain young architect's office.

And then there was the time he had eyed the intricate mass of cabling that held the massive TV tower upright. Many had ascended the 600-foot structure via the latticework of steel girders that made up the tower, but via the 4-inch thick cables that were constantly buffeted by the ever- present winds – never – until Tom completed the task that is. Unaided and without ropes, a safety harness or protective headgear he had virtually scampered up the swaying cable clad only in his ubiquitous black coat that was to become the trademark that made him instantly recognisable by all.

His climbing feats had not always been skywards. Living in a limestone area that was riddled with potholes and subterranean caverns had given him many opportunities to descend deep into the bowels of the earth. On such dangerous expeditions one would have expected Tom to equip himself a little more liberally, yet ever the free spirit he chose to rely solely on his own natural accoutrements and ability to make the hazardous descents without even so much as a flashlight. Fortunately he had been blessed with very keen eyesight that had given him a distinct advantage over most of the other cave explorers.

His slim frame had also assisted him in reaching areas where others would not dare to venture for fear of getting stuck. The only barrier to these underground adventures had been the occasional rock pool that he encountered. The simple fact was that Tom did not like water in any form; not even for drinking and milk was no doubt his preferred tipple. It was an inherited characteristic and there is little that anyone can do to override genetic influences.

As exciting as his underground explorations had been, there's little doubt that Tom preferred to experience his adrenalin rush in the open air. However he was never foolhardy with his climbing exploits – well that is not since an occasion in his younger days when youthful impetuosity had almost cost him his life. The family had gone camping deep in the countryside and had pitched their tents in the shadow of a ruined castle. Tom had been fascinated by the now crumbling walls and once fortified battlements but more so by the lofty castellated tower that to his immature mind appeared to be almost reaching the sky. Even at this young age he saw beyond the mere stone and mortar structure and searched instead for the imperfections that he knew would afford a foothold and help him scale this ancient but impressive edifice.

Dusk was falling and after a tasty supper of trout caught that very day in the stream that meandered past the campsite, Tom was ready for his climb. It proved not to difficult and soon he was perched on the highest turret, gazing at the beautiful countryside spread out below him – and then it happened. Out of nowhere the huge winged shape swooped down on young Tom. It was a female tawny owl and unbeknown to Tom she had a nest nearby and had assessed that this would be trespasser was a likely predator who would plunder her nest. The razor sharp claws brushed Tom's cheek but did not draw blood. However the shock of the unforeseen attack caused Tom to lose his hold and he tumbled inwards on to a decaying joist that was all that remained of the castle roof. The owl continued her relentless attack and despite a heroic attempt to defend himself, he was no match for the determined bird who once again dislodged him from the joist and he fell to the ground below. Fortunately his fall was broken by an accumulation of yielding mosses and pine leaf litter that had built up over countless decades and now carpeted the dark interior of the castle keep. Fortunately there were no broken bones – unfortunately it had all been to much for the rotten joist as it broke away from the wall and fell across Tom, pinning him to the ground as secure as any shackle could have done.

Luckily for him, the family heard his plaintive cries and he was rescued just as the last rays of the sun were disappearing behind the distant hills. Though shaken but not badly hurt, Tom that day learned a very salutary lesson that was to serve him well over the coming years...

There was no doubt that since then Tom had faced and conquered innumerable challenges in his lifetime. However, there was one challenge that not even this irrepressible climber could hope to gain ascendancy over and that was – old age. For the past couple of years or so he had sought no new challenges and had contented himself by revisiting old conquests and was happy enough with the realization that he could still successfully repeat earlier feats, albeit at a much reduced pace....

It was a bitterly cold day in late January when Tom attempted what was to be his final climb. Snow had fallen the previous night, carpeting the earth with a 2-inch layer, which had then frozen hard, as the temperature had plummeted to five degrees below zero – It was certainly not a day for climbing, not even for the most fearless and foolhardy of climbers – But the lofty shape had loomed large out of the wintry gloom and though draped in frozen snow, with icicles hanging like frozen washing on a line – the old flame of desire was once more rekindled in his heart.

It was an ascent that he had negotiated successfully many times in the past but never in such atrocious conditions. With the sun on his back and each foothold well defined and firm he had always considered it one of his easier climbs. Today however would be a totally different ball game. The snow had once more begun to fall and was being whipped up to near blizzard conditions by the ever-fluctuating wind, every climber's worst-case scenario as Tom began the perilous ascent. Once again he had misjudged the task before him and though he succeeded in reaching the halfway mark it was at this point that his resolve ran out.

As the last of the strength drained from his cramping limbs, Tom sensed that he was no longer alone. Muffled voices cut through the swirling snow and he realized that help was close by.

The hand reached out to grab him - but it was to late. The unfortunate and foolhardy climber lost his tenuous hold and with a mournful cry he fell from the branch – Fortunately, like all paid up member of the feline species, he landed on his feet; shook his dishevelled head; smoothed his bedraggled whiskers and hurried through the cat flap to see if dinner was ready!

Sleeping Partner!

'No single supplements available; however a sleeping partner of the same sex can be arranged.' Toby Jones read aloud from the glossy brochure that had recently been delivered at his behest. He had for many years nurtured a dream of visiting the 'Valley of The Kings' in Egypt but for a variety of reasons including the unrelenting pressure of running an ailing garden centre and a demanding spouse who believed that money not spent on adding to her considerable wardrobe was money wasted, it had remained but a dream. However, a series of unfortunate events over the past few months had allowed the dream to crystallize somewhat.

The first of these adverse events was the not so surprising collapse of the business. This was quickly followed by the exit of Mrs Jones who had been seriously attracted to the top of the range Lexus driven by the senior administrator who, like an eager vulture had picked clean the few

remaining assets of the business (The fact that he was plug ugly and bordering on being morbidly obese was neither here or there).
These were reasons enough for a sensitive soul such as Toby to become thoroughly disheartened with his lot – but there was worse to come. The increasing ferocity of his headaches he had put down to the stress he was under. However there was no doubting the result of his recent scan and he should have realized that events, good or bad, quite often come in 'threes' and his third 'slap in the kisser' turned out to be the 'daddy' of them all – an untreatable brain tumour.
His few remaining friends had expected him to crumble on receipt of such a devastating diagnosis and were somewhat surprised when he announced his lifelong ambition of visiting the land of the Pharaohs. His doctor had warned him that he considered it a rash decision, but Toby reckoned he had nothing to lose; a belief that was reinforced when he asked the time worn clichéd question, "How long have I got doc'?" and the response being another classic, "six months at the most." So what if he was bitten by an asp or trampled by a charging camel, his life expectancy reduction was neither here nor there. Somehow or other he had managed to scrape enough cash together to pay for a cheap 7-day holiday in one of the less popular resorts on the ' tourist trail', hence the 'no single supplement' clause and it was with the twin sentiments of excitement and apprehension that he boarded the plane on a bleak and sunless Monday morning in April.........

The taxi ride from Cairo airport to his somewhat seedy hotel had been hot, dusty and tiring. He was glad to escape the unrelenting heat as he stepped from the sun's unyielding glare to the relatively cool embrace of the hotel lobby. For a moment he thought he had stepped into an old film set of the 1940's classic 'Casablanca'. The rather timeworn desk was probably new at about that time and supported a potted plant, a large old-fashioned telephone and the type of register that most hotels had dispensed with years ago. This scenario was further reinforced when Toby set eyes on the concierge, who, sporting a battered red fez at least two sizes too small, was a cross between Sydney Greenstreet and Tommy Cooper.

The hammers in Toby's head had once more begun to pound and it was with some relief, when after completing the usual booking in formalities he was handed the key to his room. On entering, he was at first surprised to find that the room was already occupied by a rather slight and elderly gentleman, who turned and gave him a most endearing and ice-breaking smile of welcome.

"Sit down my friend, you must be tired after your journey." He gestured in the direction of a large and battered cane-backed chair in the corner of the sparsely furnished room. 'Gosh! It's as though he read my mind' thought Toby as he flopped down into it's inviting embrace as he realized that this was obviously his designated 'sleeping partner' for the duration of the holiday. His new companion handed him a glass of ice-cold greenish liquid that was probably a local concoction of mixed fruits and berries. Toby accepted it gratefully

and as the last drops passed his parched lips the pounding in his head subsided to almost nothing. He realized that this was the best he had felt for many months and wondered just how much the greenish potion had contributed to this new feeling of well being.
He glanced over at the somewhat rickety table in the centre of the room and was surprised to find it laden with all manner of plates and dishes, each containing a mixture of hot and cold foodstuffs that were in the main unfamiliar to him. The aroma that wafted from these assorted dishes was enough to remind him that it was several hours since his last meal and he was pleased when his new friend announced that he had taken the trouble to order a meal for the both of them.
"I do hope you will forgive my presumption of your dietary preferences Toby, but I think you will find there is enough choice here to satisfy the most pernickety of appetites." Toby had to agree that everything looked most inviting and after first thanking his new companion for his foresight in ordering the meal, proceeded to 'tuck in' to the feast laid out before him.
At the conclusion of the meal, Toby settled back into the comfort of the cane-backed chair and eyed his new companion who, although seemingly sociable enough, exuded this definite air of mystery. Many questions were forming in his mind but before he could formulate them into words his friend spoke first.
"What line of business are you in Toby." He asked enquiringly. That was the second time this stranger had addressed him by name and yet Toby was pretty sure he had not heard it from his lips. 'Probably got it from the

register' he mused dismissively. However, Toby who was normally shy and reticent, particularly about personal matters, found that with virtually no persuasion he was opening his heart completely to this perfect stranger. He told him of the failed business, the break-up with his wife and most surprisingly of all, the precarious state of his health.

The man looked searchingly into Toby's eyes, his arms across his chest, the tips of his fingers lightly drumming together – And then he spoke.

"Toby, you must not despair. It is not yet your time to depart this life neither is it written that you should remain insolvent. Look deep into your heart and you will find the will and fortitude to save your business. I believe that your wife is probably regretting her rash decision and a doctor's prognosis is not always right. I suggest you and I retire for the night and when you awake I am confident that you will see what lies before you in a different light……….."

The bed was probably the most comfortable that Toby had ever experienced and after months of intermittent sleep due to the relentless pain of the tumour, he now came round from ten hours of painless and unbroken slumber – and he felt great. He glanced across to his companion's bed and was somewhat surprised to find it both empty and apparently not even slept in. He realized that he did not even know the name of his sleeping partner but surmised that he had risen early and was probably arranging for breakfast to be served. As his eyes became accustomed to the rather gloomy interior he saw that on the table was a large glass of the strange green-coloured liquid that had tasted so refreshing and had apparently masked the pain from his tumour (which strangely enough, apart from a little 'niggle', had not bothered him since the first draught had been consumed). As he drank the ice-cold tincture, relishing the unusual and exotic flavour, he wondered as to how it could be so cold. It was at least 30 degrees C in the room and there was no sign of a refrigerator or cool box. As the last drop was drained, even that little 'niggle' had departed and he felt better than he had done for many months. He decided it was time to seek out his newfound friend and thank him for his kindness.

Sydney Greenstreet aka Tommy Cooper was seated at the desk idly swishing an ancient flywhisk. Toby was about to enquire as to the whereabouts of his sleeping partner but the 'fezed one' beat him to it.

"Ah! Mr Jones, I trust you had a restful night and we will not be charging you for sole occupancy of the room. Your designated sleeping partner was a passenger on a flight that unfortunately crashed en-route from Switzerland – It is a great calamity as there were no survivors!"

Someone To Watch Over Me!

Friday the 13th, whilst sat in the dock at Crown Court, was the day when Tiberius Ignatius Tubbs sacked his Guardian Angel. He reckoned that the many years of unfortunate incidents, not to mention the bad luck that had dogged him over the same period was enough for any mere mortal to endure. For instance how could any caring parent have saddled their offspring with such ridiculous forenames, and when combined with his family name making such an unfortunate acronym? All through his schooldays and even into later life he could never recall anybody addressing him as 'Tiberius' or 'Ignatius'. The gentler souls made do with 'Tibby' or 'Iggy' or occasionally 'Tubby'. However it was those crueller associates that took great delight in calling him by the unfortunate

acronym, which was often followed by the suffix 'head' - and he blamed it all on his GA.
The more he considered his action of ridding himself of that persistent nagging voice, the more he realized that events could not possibly get any worse if he proceeded through the remaining years of his life without that smug little do-gooder sitting on his shoulder and whispering sanctimonious rubbish in his ear. Relieved of what he considered to be his cumbersome burden, he reflected on the many times when that irritating little voice had whispered such brainless advice. There was the time when he had bullied Charlie Ponsonby-Smythe into accompanying him on a raid to Mr Saul's orchard, where the pair had stripped his prize apple trees bare. GA had advised him to come clean and accept the consequences when he knew all along that a much wiser course of action would have been to blame it all on Charlie, which of course he had done and escaped completely the beating that had ensued.
And then there was the time when he had persuaded Gilbert Snodgrass that it would be fun to peep into the girls' changing room at the school swimming gala. All had appeared to be going well until that insufferable Lucy Shufflebottom had spotted the pair of them peering over the somewhat flimsy partition. Again GA had advised him to 'come clean' but he knew that swearing that it was all Gilbert's fault for leading him astray was a much more judicious option, which of course was the action he had taken, thus escaping the wrath of Mr Ogilvey the headmaster who had administered to the gullible Gilbert twelve of the best and a thousand lines stating 'I must not

ogle naked girls' (a strange choice of wording to hand to an impressionable 15 year old – but that was Mr Ogilvey for you).

He continued with his musing and recalled some of the events that had occurred after he had departed High School for college. GA had advised English, Maths and a Science subject but after a swift glance at the accompanying curriculum's he decided that there were more meaningful (and easier) subjects to pursue such as Hospitality Management, Modern Dance or even Bird Watching (He had already become proficient at this latter art form, but I hasten to add, not of the feathered variety). He had eventually plumped for Art and Design, as no doubt he did possess some little skill in this particular field. Unfortunately as end of term exams' loomed, and despite constant promptings from GA, he realized that he was badly equipped to get anywhere near a pass mark. Still, if there had been a course for deviousness he would no doubt have gained a 'first' - and with honours to boot.

Now it so happened that Genevieve Hardcastle, the young assistant college secretary, who had developed somewhat of a 'crush' for Tiberius, had let slip that the forthcoming examination papers were to be delivered the following day. Although it had taken him to the limits of his sinister persuasive powers, he had managed to convince her that giving him sight of the Art & Design exam' paper would be no great sin and that his thanks would know no bounds. Dreaming no doubt of a night of unbridled passion, she had Foolishly acquiesced to his roguish scheme and should not have been surprised when he had made photocopies of the paper, which he had then sold onto to his more unscrupulous classmates. Naturally when the brown stuff had hit the fan, despite pleas from GA to own up, he had denied all knowledge of his implication and had shown little or no remorse when poor Genevieve had been summarily dismissed from her post.

Somehow or other, after obtaining a less than flattering university degree, and that more through cunning rather than diligence, he had obtained a position in a large multi-national company as a junior designer. There he had struck up a convenient friendship with one, Tobias Trubshaw, a fellow designer of infinite talent but little street-wise awareness. As the years passed, the pair had steadily climbed the design team ladder, thanks mainly to the genius of Tobias and the sly craftiness of Tiberius, who clung like a diseased limpet onto the coat tails of his talented partner. The pinnacle of their career advancement saw them being handed a project for the interior design of an iconic structure that was to be built in a neighbouring town.

Tobias was immediately drawn to his computer and with constant urging and prompting from his 'partner' had soon formulated designs that were far in advance of their time and it was of no surprise to anyone when the client, who had been equally impressed, had given the 'green light' for the design to be transformed into reality. GA, although realizing that the input from Tiberius had been minimal, had quietly advised him to continue on what appeared to be an acceptable path. Tiberius though had other more unscrupulous and devious plans in mind. He elected himself as chief procurer for the many expensive materials that were necessary to meet the requirements of the fabulous design. However, and true to his nature, he realized that there was money to be made from this venture. As the order forms passed through his hands, many were amended for the purchase of inferior materials and the money saved was then diverted into his own bank account.

Unfortunately one of his nefarious decisions involved the purchase of flameproof cladding. A quick scan of the materials catalogue revealed a material that was virtually identical but without the flame proofing properties and less than a third of the price. Although GA had advised him that this unholy meddling would all end in tears he took no notice of this prudent advice.......

The opening ceremony of the prestigious building was going well until the powerful spotlights in the magnificent assembly hall were switched on. The heat generated by these intense lights was such that any adjacent materials, if not flame proofed, would be subject to eventual combustion – I think you can probably draw your own conclusions as to what happened next.

The building was gutted and people were lucky to escape with their lives. The reason for the blaze was quickly established and the accusing finger of responsibility was initially pointed unerringly at both Tobias and Tiberius. Once again Tiberius did his utmost to pin the blame on his partner – but on this occasion he found that his luck had run out as it was quickly established that it was his signature alone on the invoices for the inferior materials.

And so it was on that fateful Friday that Tiberius had found himself sitting alone in the dock of the local Crown

Court. Even at this late hour his deceitful thought processes were actively engaged in seeking ways to wriggle out of the mess in which he now found himself. He was finding the task somewhat difficult due to the constant nagging from GA on his shoulder.
"What will it take to get rid of you?" He muttered in exasperation. "Go on! – Clear off! – I don't need your stupid advice," he added vehemently. To his surprise the insistent little voice was stilled. 'If only I'd realized how simple it was to get shut of you I would have done it years ago,' he said to himself.

As the trial began, Tiberius was not overly surprised to learn that Tobias Trubshaw was to be the chief prosecution witness. However, he was somewhat taken aback when he saw Lucy Shufflebottom giving him 'evils' from the jury benches. He grew even more perturbed to see both Gilbert Snodgrass and Genevieve Hardcastle sitting close by her. His resolve then deserted him completely when the court usher bade them all stand to receive the presiding judge for the trial, one Charles Ponsoby-Smythe QC.
"OMG!" he muttered to himself. "They've got me bang to rights. What do I do now?" But answer – there came none! – And why?
"Well he fired me didn't he? And now I'm off for my next assignment. I only hope that this time I get somebody who will listen to me!"

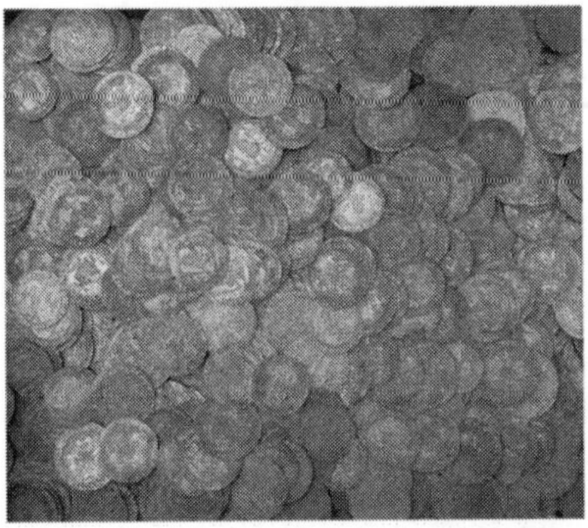

A Fistful of – Dendraspis?

Adam was terribly unlucky. At least that was his own pithy self-appraisal as to the rotten cards that life had been dealing him over his 23 years searching for that ever-elusive pot of gold at the end of the rainbow. However, rainbows had not appeared very often in his relatively young life never mind the theoretical riches that supposedly lay at its terminus. Truth be known, rainbows have never been exactly prolific in the sleazy bars and seedy snooker halls, which had been Adam's haunts of choice since leaving (make that expelled from) college. Indeed the only 'good' thing that had ever passed over the threshold of his indolent and mundane life had been Eve; a brassy blonde of similar age to himself. She also frequented the establishments favoured by Adam and their relationship had been cemented on that fateful evening a couple of years ago when he had helped her rifle through the pockets of an unlucky punter she had enticed down the litter strewn alley that ran behind one of the aforementioned bars.

For a time, such pernicious activities had been the main source of their joint income, yet the few pounds that such nefarious activities brought in never quite matched their lofty ambitions – That is until one of Eve's more talkative 'clients', a locksmith from a neighbouring town had babbled on about fitting a load of security devices for the crippled guy who lived in the big old house down by the river. "To ensure that no one could get at his 'dendraspis' so he said" Eve was about to ask him about the dendraspis when his tenth shot of 'Jack Daniels' consumed that evening finally caught up with him and he slipped noiselessly to the floor. 'My lucky night' mused Eve as she expertly frisked the unfortunate but now comatose locksmith. Not only did she find a wallet containing a couple of hundred pounds but also a set of keys carrying a label that proclaimed that they belonged to 'Riverside House' – The very residence wherein lay the mysterious dendraspis.........

"Don't ask me," said Adam sullenly when later that night Eve had questioned him about the dendraspis. "Never heard of 'em, though come to think of it they do sound like some ancient foreign currency or other – Yea! I'm sure that's what they are – old foreign coins and probably worth a fortune. The old geezer who lives there probably has a collection and that locksmith guy was obviously upping his security arrangements. Gee! If only we could get in, we would probably come out with a fortune." It was at that point that Eve dangled the house keys in front of Adam's unbelieving eyes............

The night was dark and moonless with a vapid mist rising languidly from the river that flowed past the old house as Adam and Eve crept stealthily up to the sturdy oaken front door. The house itself was also in total darkness as Adam eventually found the key that fitted the rather old-fashioned lock. It turned noiselessly and 30 seconds later the scheming pair were inside.

"Where now?" hissed Eve as her eyes grew accustomed to the gloom.

"How the blazes do I know?" answered Adam aggressively. "We'll just have to search round until we come to a locked room or summat. He's hardly likely to leave his dendraspis just lying about for anybody to nick now is he?" The pair went carefully from room to room, looking for evidence of a safe or strongbox but found – nothing. That is until they reached the rear of the house and saw before them a huge and ornate typical Victorian conservatory. Tentatively Adam tried the door – It was locked!

As he searched the ring for the appropriate key, a shrill voice rang out behind him.

"I wouldn't do that if I were you!" The voice belonged to an elderly looking gentleman who was seated in a wheelchair.

"Where the hell did you come from?" queried Adam in a state of shock.

"I've been here all the time. I often sit in the dark as bright lights hurt my tired old eyes, but I say to you again, do not

enter the conservatory," replied the occupant of the wheelchair. Adam, realizing that the man was practically helpless, quickly regained his courage.
"And who is going to stop me?" he sneered revelling in the old guy's obvious infirmity.
"Yea!" Added Eve. "And we know all about your stash of dendraspis and I think you've just told us where they are," she added triumphantly.
"Ah yes, my 'stash' of dendraspis as you call it. Never actually thought they could be considered a stash, but then again........."
"Quit stalling," interrupted Adam angrily. "Just tell us where we can find them and we won't hurt you."
"Well you're certainly warm and if you go through the conservatory door you will find them all around you."
"Wot! Just lying around?" queried Eve, a note of scepticism in her voice.
"They may be difficult to spot at first but I assure you they are there alright."
"I'm getting bored with these stupid riddles," bellowed Adam as he located the key to the conservatory. "I'm gonna open the door and push you through and you can show us what we've come for."
"Very well," answered the old guy. "But I warn you now you may live to regret it."
"You'll be the one regretting things if you keep yapping your nonsense," responded Adam as he guided the wheelchair through the now open door.
The atmosphere inside the conservatory was stifling – hot and humid, taking away the breath of the two miscreants

but seemingly having little effect on the wheelchair occupant.
"So, where's these bleedin' dendraspis then?" demanded a somewhat irate Adam. "I can't see anything in this gloom."
"Oh don't worry – I assure you they are all around us – but listen – perhaps you can hear them."
"What the hell is the 'nutter' going on about? You can't hear coins."
"Coins my dear! I'm afraid you have been very much misinformed. There are no coins here – but then again there is an abundance of coils."
"Talk sense you old fool," screamed Adam. I don't care what you call them we just want whatever valuables you have in here – and Eve stop messing about with them plants; it's scary enough in here."
"It isn't me Adam," responded Eve. There must be someone else in here."
The old guy let out a wicked cackle as he joyously informed them that indeed there was someone – or rather something else in the conservatory; that for which they were seeking – dendraspis – or to be more exact - dozens of them.
The floor in front of them became a living green carpet of - snakes, and all slithering in their direction.
"So Adam and Eve, you wanted my dendraspis or to give them their non-latin name, Black Mambas, probably the most venomous and certainly most aggressive snake on the African continent. One bite usually causes an agonizing death within minutes. Oh dear! You've suddenly gone all quiet. Perhaps you're thinking of my welfare?

Well don't you worry now, after fifty years of dealing with them I am now immune to their venom – but as for you two........" But the pair of would-be robbers had not heard the final words. With adrenalin now pumping through every vein they fled through the still open door, the hideous laughter of the old guy ringing in their ears as they finally made it to the car they had parked in a lay-by close to the snake infested house.

The panic in their breasts slowly subsided as they drove towards more familiar territory. At first the road had appeared deserted and Adam was somewhat surprised to see in the rear-view mirror the twin headlights of a vehicle that was approaching from behind.

"Oh – oh! Looks like we're been followed. Bet the silly old sod has called the cops. Have a closer look Eve and see if you can tell if it's the fuzz." Eve turned round to comply with her boyfriend's instruction and found herself staring – not into headlights - but rather the cold calculating eyes of - a Black Mamba. Although the old guy had given them some information about the dendraspis family, he had omitted to inform them of one very important fact – that they can move as fast as a human can run and this one had obviously given chase. The scream of abject terror had barely reached her trembling lips before the mamba sank its venom-laden fangs deep into the soft flesh of her rouged cheek. In her death throes she clutched with inhuman strength at Adam, causing him to loose control of the car. It veered from the road and splashed into the murky waters of the river.

As the last faltering bubbles reached the surface, an old man in a wheelchair was the sole witness to the demise of the wicked duo. He smiled inwardly as he mused that they were not the first Adam and Eve to fall victims to a serpent.

OK! So maybe I'm pushing on the door of plagiarism – Well yes, I must admit that the inspiration for this little chiller came from the pen of perhaps one of the greatest writers of Victorian horror stories; an era that abounded with tellers of such blood curdling tales. W. W. Jacobs was certainly up there with the likes of Edgar Allan Poe, Mary Shelley and not forgetting good old boy – Bram Stoker. I would like to think that if W. W had written a sequel to 'The Monkey's Paw' then perhaps it would have read something like this........

The Monkey's Other Paw!

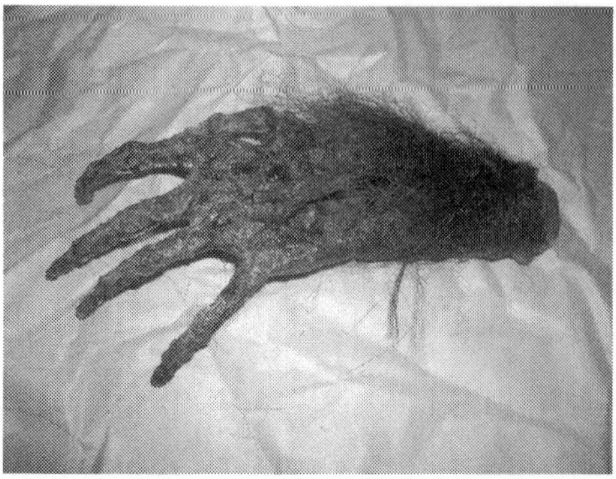

(With humble apologies to W W Jacobs, who wrote the original 'Monkey's Paw' story)

The rain lashed remorselessly against the stout walls of the cosy hostelry as interminable gusts of wind blew down the wide pub chimney, fanning the dying embers once more into flickering flame. Through the rain-spattered windows came the watery glow of the festive lights, strung along Lincoln's near deserted streets, each bulb struggling valiantly in a desperate endeavour to lighten the pervading gloom.
The oak-studded front door was suddenly thrown open, whereupon the inclement season did its best to suck the warmth from the snug interior.
"Shut that bloody door", bawled the landlord from behind the bar; the few hardy souls who had braved the

elements on such a foul evening obviously acquiesced with the sternly delivered command as they gave cursory glances at the latest arrivals. Dripping water from brightly coloured anoraks stood three young men, who were appreciably relieved to have escaped, albeit temporarily, the wrath of such inhospitable weather. Concerned with their sodden appearance, the gruff but kindly landlord bade them remove their coats and sit by the fire, whose heat generating capability he enhanced by the addition of two chunky logs that were stacked neatly in the ash-strewn grate.

It is well documented that young blood soon warms and within minutes, Tom, the tallest of the trio was at the bar ordering three half shandies.

'Bloody students', muttered the landlord to him self as he fulfilled the order. 'They'll probably make 'em last all night as well,' he mumbled. Still on a night such as this he was glad of all the customers he could get, however frugal they may be.

It was the start of the Christmas holidays and the nearby university campus was virtually deserted. The Halls of Residence, that usually rang, day and night, with the voices of energetic students were for once uncommonly quiet. Those who had not already departed were preparing to do so and an hour from now the area would be as still and quiet as the grave.

"What time's your train?" Richard enquired of Harry.

"7-15pm, platform two," Harry responded. "And yours and Tom's?"

"Ten minutes later; platform one," replied Richard.

As though he had read the landlord's thoughts, Tom interjected by saying, "Think we can make these last an hour or so then?" as he placed each brimming glass before its eager recipient. The young men chuckled together as they took their first tentative sips of the golden liquid.

It was at that moment that they realized they were being scrutinized. No, not by the landlord, he had long given up on any ideas of making a fortune out of the grinning trio. The individual who was now staring at them so boldly was seated at the other side of the fireplace. It was Harry who first noticed this unsolicited attention as he alerted his companions to the situation.

"What's old almond eyes goggling at?" said Tom rather ungraciously. It was plain to observe that their inquisitor was indeed of oriental origin but neither Chinese or Japanese, more Malayan or East Indian. He was also of that perplexing ilk where it was virtually impossible to ascertain his age. He could have been forty or sixty or anywhere in between. Only his slightly hunched shoulders and work-worn hands hinted that he might even be older. His shabby clothing had a hint of the sea about it and Tom was reminded of the archaic term of 'Lascar' for such a person. Richard, always the attentive one, noticed that 'Larry', as they had unceremoniously christened him, was nursing an all but empty spirit glass. Anxious to show the face of British hospitality to the elderly fellow, who held their gaze so intently, he enquired, "Would you like a top-up sir?" The man's face appeared to crack as he broke into the most almighty grin and in meticulous English

replied that a small rum would be most gratefully received and no doubt faithfully applied.
The old man appeared to take the receipt of the drink as an invitation to join the threesome and so with much bowing and fussing he placed himself on a stool with just a small table between them on which he placed his drink.
"You have shown much kindness to me young sirs, a kindness that I despaired of ever finding in your cold country and for your courtesy I would like to offer you something in return." As he spoke he reached towards a grimy duffel bag that he had deposited on the floor beside him.
"You've not got the 'Koh-I-Noor in there have you?" enquired Tom with a mischievous wink in the direction of his pals.
"Ah so you know of the great diamond so beloved by the Mogul emperors learned sir. Alas I carry no such treasures but what I have, so I believe, surpasses all earthly jewels."
"It's the elixir of life," said Harry as all three students warmed to the banter.
"Would that it were," responded their uninvited guest. "If that were so I would drain such a draught to regain my own youth and return once more to the seven seas that I traversed for many a long year. Yet it could be said that what I am about to show you transcends even that much sought after miracle of which you speak." With that he opened the duffel bag and withdrew a small black wooden box covered with intricate carvings and certainly of eastern origin. He appeared to press the eye of a beautifully detailed dragon, which in turn caused the ornate lid to flip open. There, nestling on a bed of red

velvet, was what at first glance appeared to be a rabbit's foot. Closer scrutiny however revealed that although it was without doubt an animal's appendage, it was certainly not of the 'bunny' family.

The fascinated trio looked in unison at their newfound companion and in anticipation of the question that hovered on their inquisitive lips he remarked, "It is a very special monkey's paw!" Richard was the first to burst into a fit of uncontrollable laughter, which was quickly taken up by his comrades.
"By golly Larry," he remonstrated, using the somewhat derogatory name by which they had christened him. "You nearly had us going there. You'll be telling us next that you went to sea with W W Jacobs and that you pinched this relic from a Sergeant-Major Morris." The laughter grew in intensity as the three Classic English students poured scorn and ridicule on their hapless victim. They above all certainly knew of the classic horror story penned in the early years of the last century and were now convinced that their erstwhile 'friend' was in some way attempting to 'con' them.

"And I suppose that on receipt of a ridiculous sum of money, we can all use it to make a wish," added Tom, still chortling. The mood of the Lascar suddenly darkened and with unrestrained fury he hissed, "You have insulted me most gravely and I am appalled that such ostensible English gentlemen should turn out to possess the manners of swine and the integrity of serpents. I was about to reward your generosity with tales of this magical artefact, but instead I give it to you," and then with a satanic grin he added, "and may it do you all much good." He tossed the mummified paw onto the table; carelessly rammed the ornate box back into his duffel bag and with muffled curses, uttered in a strange dialect, he shuffled out of the bar and into the wild and unwelcoming night.

"Well! We certainly touched a raw nerve there," said Harry.

"You don't suppose that there's anything in that old story?" remarked Tom.

"Come on Tom," responded Richard, smiling somewhat at his friend's naivety. "You'll be expecting Santa to come down the chimney next!" Richard and Harry laughed even louder at this somewhat teasing remark, although Tom retained his air of uncertainty.

"My God, He really thinks that making a wish while holding that flea-bitten relic will actually make it come true."

"No! Of course I don't," he responded with little conviction in his voice. "But don't forget that old adage that there are more things in heaven and earth than this world dreams of."

"No wonder you're struggling with your literature course you berk, you can't even quote Macbeth correctly," replied Richard.

"Your not exactly covering yourself with literary glory," interjected Harry with an air of learned superiority. "It comes from Hamlet actually and the correct quotation is 'There are more things in heaven and earth, Horatio, than are dreamt of in your philosophy'"

"Come on lads! Lets not get all semantic about it. Look! I'll put the issue to bed once and for all," replied Richard and with that he took the paw in his hand and with great sombreness and before his companions could stop him, he pronounced with mock solemnity, "I wish for free beer for the rest of my life." For a brief second the lights in the pub dipped; the thing in his hand convulsed and with a start Richard flung the paw back onto the table.
"Bloody hell," screamed Richard in some alarm. "Did you see that? His two pals were almost collapsing in paroxysms of laughter at Richard's obvious distress.
"You stupid pillock," snorted Harry through floods of mirth. "You really have let this get to you haven't you? The lights dipped because we are in the middle of a storm, and whatever you think you felt – well, it's just the product of an overworked imagination. Give it here – I'll prove it to you. Now then what do I really need? – I know – infinite knowledge, or at least enough to get me to the third year of this English Classics degree. So what should I wish for then? I've got it – I wish I had a bigger brain." Whether by coincidence or not, but again the steady lights flickered; the paw twisted in Harry's hand but there was no way he was going to let on as his mates, Tom in particular, gawped apprehensively at him. With a self-satisfied smirk he laid the paw lightly on the table and sat back.
"Well, I don't feel any wiser yet," he remarked.
"And I don't see much free beer coming my way," smiled Richard. This last rather rueful comment broke the tension that had been building and again the trio laughed out loudly at the seeming absurdity of the situation.

“Come on Tom! Your turn,” said Richard, handing the paw over to him.
Now the landlord and a couple of his regulars had been watching this strange drama unfold. With a sly wink to his cronies, the landlord pulled a pint of Guinness; walked across the room and placed it in front of the somewhat bemused Richard.
“There you go son. Have this one on the house. It’s been worth it just watching the antics of the three of you.”
My God! It’s working,” shrieked Harry in mock terror, his face contorted with unrestrained laughter. Richard, never being one to look a gift horse in the mouth, thanked the landlord and took a deep draught of the dark liquid.
Now it would be logical to assume that the spigot tap from the dispenser had been accidentally dislodged when the landlord had pulled the pint – wouldn’t it? Well by accident or magic it mattered not a jot when it stuck firmly in Richard’s windpipe as he fell to the floor gasping for air after that first greedy guzzle. This normally would have been the sole issue for concern to all and sundry except that to add to the general mayhem that now ensued, Harry was rising from his seat, both hands clutched to his head. The area around his temples seemed to bulge unnaturally and a thin trickle of blood could be seen dribbling from his nose and ears. He too then fell to the floor with the top of his skull pulsating ominously.
Tom, in abject terror, surveyed the nightmarish scene that was unfolding before him. As his erstwhile friends screamed and thrashed on the floor before him, the overwhelming instinct of survival kicked in. He blubbered uncontrollably and moaned softly,

"Oh dear God! I wish I was back within the university walls." There was a rushing sound, like the rising of a great wind and Tom felt himself being carried aloft by unseen forces before he momentarily blacked out. Seconds later all was quiet – deathly quiet. As Tom slowly regained his senses he realized he could see nothing. It was as though he was entombed in a stygian darkness. However his keen sense of smell identified the bookish odour that always struck him whenever he entered the University library, a structure that had been totally transformed from a century old warehouse. The fear that had built inside him quickly subsided as he realized where he was. And of course it was dark as by now the building would be deserted and all the lights switched off. Still, that shouldn't present too much of a problem. All he needed to do was find his bearings, get to the nearest phone and ring for someone to let him out.

He attempted to move his arm but was surprised when it met resistance. The same happened as he tried to move his other arm; similarly his legs also appeared to be encased and immovable. In fact whichever way he attempted to move his now cramping body, he found that apart from an inch or two the feat was nigh impossible. A terrifying realization swiftly dawned as he recalled the precise words he had uttered whilst clutching that infernal paw, wishing himself back within the university walls – And that's exactly where he now found himself – In the cavity space between the refurbished walls of the library...

No one heard the fearful screams that echoed round the deserted building that night. Screams that lessened in volume as each seemingly endless hour passed by. No one that is except perhaps for the lone hunched figure that shuffled past the shadowy edifice, carrying a rather battered duffel bag and softly humming a tune that was distinctly oriental!

Who Are We Having For Dinner?

It had amused Manfred when, nestling among the many bills and assorted junk mail that he had received that morning, he came across the organ donor card. *'Have A Heart'* it announced in bold roman face, followed by the plea, *'But When You're Done Then Pass It On'*. He chuckled to himself at the rather witty sentiment as with a flourish he signed it 'Manfred Hay'. Now you may speculate at the reason for his hilarity at the idea of completing an organ donor card. Surely this was quite a serious commitment and not one that would promote jocularity for most normal people. But then again, Manfred could never be described as being one of life's 'most normal people' – you see – and not to put too fine a point on it – he was a cannibal! Oh! Not your run of the mill, knock 'em on the head, stuff 'em in the pot cannibal,

Manfred was too much of a gourmet and connoisseur of fine dining to even consider practising the crude abominations of his savage ancestors. He preferred instead the more subtle and gentile approach of issuing invitations to dine, without informing the recipients of such polite invitations that they were more than likely to be the main course on the menu.

The refinement however didn't end there. He was, if nothing else, rather fastidious about his dietary arrangements, which also made him quite choosy as to which parts of his victims anatomy he actually preferred. It is now well documented that although he was quite partial to the odd rack of ribs or even noisette of armpit and would certainly never turn his nose up at fricassee of foot, there was no doubting that if the truth be known he was really a 'liver, heart and lights' man. The carrying therefore of the donor card was doubly amusing, as it gave the whole business of recycling a brand new perspective. He giggled when he thought of himself as probably the only potential 'green' cannibal in existence.

However, laughter had not come easily to Manfred in recent weeks. Despite endless re-runs of 'Silence of the Lambs' and an unsuccessful attempt at growing fava beans and an absolute disaster when he tried to brew his own Chianti (the airing cupboard will never be the same again). The truth was that despite his futile efforts at finding a suitable hobby or pastime, nothing had succeeded. He had of late grown quite despondent in the knowledge that he was fast running out of 'friends', or come to think of it, even passing acquaintances that he could invite round for a 'bite'. The hard facts though were undeniably apparent. Whilst he continued to practice the rather unsociable habit of dining off them rather than with them, he would sooner or later run out of prospective 'guests'. He ruminated that the only time they had been known to 'return' was either in the form of indigestion or flatulence.

But now a significant birthday was fast approaching and so frantic had Manfred become for a taste, nay a surfeit of his erstwhile staple diet of 'long pig' that he had in sheer desperation sent beautifully crafted invitations to both Anthony Hopkins and Jodie Foster, inviting them for what he described as 'sharing the experience of a truly memorable meal'. Of course such invitations had been dispatched more in hope than expectation and Manfred was less than surprised when both celebrities had rejected his offer, pleading prior engagements. By now he was at least ten degrees below 'utter desperation mode' as he frantically thumbed through his personnel listings diary. It was on the last page that he came upon the scrawled entry 'Alice'. Alice, he mused who the f—lipping heck is Alice? Then it returned to him like a rather nasty boomerang. 'Dearest' Alice was or rather had been his one-time mother-in-law, who he held in somewhat lower esteem than foot rot or bubonic plague.

His initial reaction on seeing her name was to dismiss the absurd thought completely. However the more he thought about it the more inviting the prospect became.

Alice! The woman who had brought him nothing but heartache and misery – and that was before she had learned of his rather unusual dietary delectations. What a fulfilling payback to make the old bag eat her own disparaging words – before they had actually left her mouth. The more thought he gave it, the more pleasing the prospect became. With shaking hand, accompanied by much licking of expectant lips, he penned the somewhat insincere invitation to his one-time mother-in-law inviting her round for what he had described to her as a rather special birthday treat. Exactly who would be 'treated' he had purposely omitted to elaborate upon.

Imagine his surprise when she returned the RSVP portion of the formal invitation duly completed - and in the affirmative.
"Greedy old cow," he muttered to himself. "Thinks she's going to get a free meal out of me does she! Have I a surprise waiting for her." It would be reasonable to say that there was little love lost between the two of them. In fact the only time he had ever seen her smile was the day her daughter had finally walked out on him. (There had been many good reasons for her eventual departure, but it's strange how sometimes it's the most insignificant of issues that finally tips the scales - She had never been able to come to terms with his quite appalling halitosis)-----.

The ageing flesh had been tougher than he had anticipated, but then again he was quite philosophic enough to realise that he was in no position to be 'picky'. It had been quite some time since he had dined 'Homo

Sapiens' and he had been determined not to leave the slightest morsel. As he pushed aside the now empty plate, he was already beginning to regret his rash gourmandising. The thighs had been stringy; the arms barely edible and as for the breast meat! – Well perhaps the less said about that the better. As for his usual favourite cuts – one could only describe these as being truly 'offal' (sic). There was now little doubt that mother – damn her tough old hide – was fighting back, with a vengeance. He felt the bile rise in his gullet and was only half way to the bathroom when he tripped over the somewhat prophetic though quite ghastly reproduction of Da Vinci's 'The Last Supper', which mother had brought him as a birthday gift; fell onto the knife he was still holding and promptly severed his carotid artery – In less than a minute his life blood ceased to flow and he was quite dead.

The police at first were somewhat suspicious when they investigated the incident scene. It was obvious even to the untrained eye that more than one person had been in the apartment that evening. But despite a meticulous search of the premises they could find no evidence of a third party (perhaps if they had paid a little more attention to the waste disposal unit they would have realised that most animal carcasses don't include painted fingernails). The attending doctor was undoubtedly thorough. He had quickly located the organ donor card while Manfred was still warm and it was only a matter of hours before his 'vitals' were speeding on their way to a private clinic that specialized in human organ transplants -----------.

"My name is Clive. My surname – well, it's almost unpronounceable and not really important. Apparently its roots originate from among the Carib Indian tribes, who as well as been the indigenous people of the Caribbean Islands were more infamously known for their cannibalistic tendencies – but I digress. I had been on the organ waiting list for many months before hearing that a perfect match had been found for my quite rare blood group. I am informed that I am almost fully recovered from the multi organ transplant that I have recently undergone. The first successful one in the world apparently. Although I feel well enough, somehow I am not myself. I came in here a confirmed vegetarian, despite my ancient links to a more carnivorous diet, yet I keep suffering these horrible visions of blood-running carcasses belonging to – well I'm not really sure, although they do look vaguely familiar. The worst part however is that the harrowing experience is becoming less and less repugnant to me. I keep getting this uncontrollable urge to invite everyone I see around for dinner, and for some inexplicable reason I've just signed a cheque 'Manfred Hey'.

I am informed that it's 'liver and onions' for dinner tonight and already I'm drooling – and it's not at the thought of onions! My yearning for nut cutlet is no more. My erstwhile favourite dish of spinach flan garnished with pistachios now sounds positively revolting. But then again,

I don't half fancy a nurse, or a doctor, or even old Harry in the next bed!"

Trick or Treat?

Like the majority of postmen dread the onset of Christmas and all the extra work involved, I embrace similar feelings about Halloween. Now don't get me wrong; I admit that the establishment is kept pretty busy throughout the year as lawlessness is certainly on the rise throughout the land, but Halloween does tend to stretch our staffing resources to near breaking point and as a boss who can generally delegate the day-to-day duties to lesser minions, I find

that come October 31st then I have little choice but to join the front line personnel. Still, I'm not complaining. It helps keep them on their toes to see how senior members of the force cope with the call-outs and issues that inevitably arise with the Halloween rabble-rousers.
And as I trudged up old Pendle Hill in answer to the latest appeal, the swirling mist forming droplets on my cape, I mused on the kind of welcome I would receive. It's quite amusing really to imagine the reaction when the various gatherings of so-called witches, wizards and once a year Satanists clap eyes on me and the junior officers coming over the brow of the summit. No doubt some will be prancing around in various stages of undress, whilst others less animated will huddle round their ancient scrolls and books, chanting invocations that they hope will conjure up denizens from the underworld – And then we appear!
The first reaction of these sad little gatherings is usually one of blind panic as they realize that the acts they have been performing, if not actually against the law are certainly frowned upon by the vast majority of the law-abiding and God fearing population. The second is generally a futile attempt to flee the scene as they anticipate being 'taken in' for their depraved behaviour, which to be fair is the usual course of action we adopt anyway. Oh we've had our many critics over the years for this seemingly over the top action. Another force (which sees itself superior to ours) has attempted to persuade us to adopt a more humanitarian approach to this annual debacle. But as I pointed out to their chief, it was pointless pussyfooting around as the majority of

miscreants would be performing exactly the same sacrilegious rites the following year – They never seem to learn.

He then had a go at us for our sentencing procedures. He considered them far to extreme and would appear to the poor damned souls involved as almost an eternity. Well I soon put him right on that one. It really was for their own good that they were incarcerated with their own kind as who in a god-fearing society would welcome a devil worshiper in their midst? Still we beg to differ on this one and no doubt we will continue to act on our own tenets and beliefs for many years to come.

However, I digress and so back to the matter in hand. I was now almost at the top of the last steep incline and I held up my hand to halt the advance of the more than eager backup forces who accompanied me; their numbers forming an almost perfect corral around the cavorting ensemble on the summit. It could have been quite a daunting and intimidating sight to more sensitive souls, seeing these apparently fine upstanding individuals; the very pillars of human society, engaging in what they consider to be sacrilegious and devilish practices in an effort to conjure up denizens from the underworld or with a bit of luck perhaps 'Old Nick' himself – Fortunately we in the team had seen it all before and even the sacrifice of an old flea-bitten goat, whose ancient blood was now flowing copiously across the naked body of a local virgin (are there any left around Pendle?) failed to promote even the flicker of an emotion among us hardened veterans of many similar campaigns.

I glanced around for the leader of the sorry group – Oh yes, there always has to be a leader; an antichrist; a High Priest who likes to think that he and Satan are on nodding terms and if his foolish disciples follow his lead then the riches of the world can be theirs for the taking – Oh Boy! Could I tell them different! It did not take long to single him out, as he was a pretty archetypical example of the breed. Short, fat, sweating profusely despite the season and lateness of the hour and naked as a jaybird as he cavorted obscenely before his adoring audience. Why on earth such misguided individuals believe that this sort of display makes them more appealing to demonic forces I will never quite understand.
Close by the cavorting one was another motley crew of ill-matched individuals who were chanting in strange tongues what they believed was an irresistible command for the Prince of Darkness and all the terrifying and unspeakable fiends of Hell to arise and wrest control of Earth from He who denies unalloyed pleasure and riches to his constrained subjects – Oh! If it were only that simple I mused.
The obscene chanting rose to a crescendo and dashed my reveries once more, reminding me just what we were there for. I glanced quickly around and saw that my loyal band of aides were poised and waiting for my signal to reveal ourselves to the perverted rabble, whose debauched and beseeching cries were loud and horrifying enough to call the very devil from his lair (which to be fair I suppose was their primary objective anyway).
Fortunately my subordinates and I were all well practised at breaking up such ungodly displays as let's face it; we

have been at it for more years than I care to recall and although I say it myself we have been pretty successful in fulfilling our obligations. I remember well that year we were summoned at Stonehenge. It was probably one of the largest gatherings of so-called Satanists for many a year. We were so stretched in the field that night that we were forced to call up conscripts that had just recently completed their basic training prior to being drafted into what became known as the special division. However, and despite attempted disruption by a few pesky Druids, the somewhat 'green' and unproven recruits soon grasped what was expected of them and by midnight the whole sorry bunch had been rounded up – Gosh! We certainly made things hot for them that Halloween night.

But again I digress. The witching hour is almost upon us and there is still lots to do before each and every solitary soul is within our grasp. I sense that every eye is focused on me, waiting for the signal to reveal our presence. I see no reason to hesitate any longer and with a bellow the signal is given. From their various hiding places my loyal subordinates break cover. For just a split second there is a deathly hush on the hilltop and then of course all hell breaks loose. Within minutes the majority of sorry transgressors are rounded up. I spy a few bloodied heads among the detained but put it down to over enthusiasm from my boys. A few nimble souls are still attempting to evade capture but it is a useless gesture as just like the famed 'Mounties' we always get our man (and women as well).

All is quiet again apart from the odd moan and sob from those in the constrained mob who can't quite come to

terms with what has just happened. A mournful cry rings out – 'Mam!' A desperate plea to the Almighty pierces the still night air - but I fear that neither mummy dear nor any god can offer much comfort to these poor damned souls that are now herded into my presence so that they can see first hand the personage that has answered their frantic calls.
Despite my exceedingly long time in the position, I still find it difficult to get my head round the total and abject fear and despair that my eventual presence induces. I mean come on folks – If you will climb Pendle Hill on Halloween and exhort the devil and all his crew to enter your midst then what can you expect? There are rules you know and such calls must be addressed by the powers that be. So why all the excessive screaming and shouting; the beating of breasts and tearing out of hair when I finally reveal my true image? On reflection, I think it could possibly be a combination of my blood-red eyes, cloven hooves and blackened horns that promote the initial shrieks of horror, although I am told it is more likely to be the swishing of the terrifying forked tail that ultimately induces the loudest screams and descent into total mental breakdown as the ground beneath them gapes wide to give them their first sight of the fiery furnace – Their new home for all eternity!

Honest Injun - It Will Turn Colder

It gets extremely cold in the North American state of Montana; up near to the Canadian border. Even in the mildest winter the mercury can drop to many degrees past freezing. The local inhabitants of this vast yet sparsely populated state have even devised a unique and light-hearted grading system for their severe weather systems. There is COLD, VERY COLD and GREAT SHIVERING POLAR BEARS!

However, the people accept this annual encumbrance with great stoicism and at every fall they can be found making all the preparations necessary to ensure that the approaching season finds them as prepared as possible to meet the pending tribulations. Although cold weather is guaranteed every winter, it can be quite difficult to predict just what degree of chilliness to expect. Over the past few years, the good people of the township of Browning have placed great store in the daily weather forecasts provided by their local KBWG radio station. More often than not, the station's long-term predictions had been uncannily accurate, thanks in the main to their chief meteorologist Jack Clancy. For years Jack's colleagues at the station had been a mite envious of his particular knack of forecasting cold weather, particularly as his success rate at predicting other forms of climatic conditions were no greater than theirs – That is of course before that fateful winter in the early 50's when he got it hopelessly and disastrously wrong.

Jack no longer works at KBWG as a weather forecaster, in fact Jack does very little of anything these days apart from propping up the bar at Icks Place in downtown Browning, telling his poignant story to anyone with the time and inclination to listen. It was there, in my early days as a cub journalist for the 'Glacier Reporter', that I first met him, sitting all hunched up on a high-legged stool, with a hang-dog expression and lifeless rheumy eyes, staring vacantly at an empty bottle of 'Bud'. Possessing what I optimistically imagined was a 'nose' for an interesting story; I offered to replenish his drink whilst enquiring as to the reason for his obvious melancholy state.

"Well son", he began wearily, " When you've gone from hero to zero in the space of one short winter, it's hard to be anything but sorrowful fer a once proud fella like me." I sensed a possible scoop and urged him to continue. "Twelve consecutive years I got it right on the nose, then on the wretched thirteenth my luck kinda ran out." I begged him to continue, my journalistic curiosity by now well and truly stirred. "Jack the ace forecaster they called me in these parts. Nearly allus got it right when I told 'em what sort of winter to expect and boy, did they appreciate it. Gonna be a hard one I'd tell 'em every morning in my weather slot down at the KWBG, so get those wood stocks piled high and the heating oil ordered pronto. Sure 'nuff I would mostly be right and the folks sure were mighty grateful fer what they took to be my uncanny skill. Truth be known though boy, I did cheat a little. Oh yea I could make the usual assumptions from pressure diagrams, precipitation factors and wind directions and the likes, but I had one little trick up my sleeve that no one else at the station ever cottoned on to.

Just a mile or so past the town limits was a patch of high ground, which overlooked the Blackfeet Indian reservation. Each day as winter approached, I made it my business to visit that high ground and there, with the aid of my trusty binoculars, I could see right into the heart of the community. You might ask as to why a well-established forecaster the likes o' Jack Clancy would want to go prying on the Injuns every morning prior to making his broadcast – well I'll tell yer. Those Injuns were a canny bunch, having lived in these parts for hundreds of years. They knew all the signs as to what weather to expect and then reacted accordingly. They allus kept a fair to middling stock of wood from October onwards, but if it looked like it was gonna be 'ceptionally cold they would send out extra foraging parties to add to the stockpile.

On the winter in question the initial stockpile looked purty impressive and so my forecast on that momentous day was to prepare for a harder than average winter. The following day as I took my place on the bluff overlooking the reservation, I was somewhat concerned at the heightened activity. It was usually the older kids in the camp and a few of the elderly men who did the wood gathering but on this particular day I reckoned that about fifty percent of the tribe were setting out to gather fuel. My concern arose because all official meteorological data indicated a milder than usual season in prospect. However, what did we newly arrived white folk know about the local weather compared with the accumulated knowledge and wisdom of Native Americans?

My forecast that day duly reflected my latest observations as I told my loyal audience that despite rumours to the contrary, this winter was going to be exceptionally harsh. The next morning, as once again I trained my glasses on the encampment, I was amazed to see a good seventy percent of the residents preparing to scour the countryside for even more wood. With mounting excitement, I confidently announced over the airwaves that it was looking likely to be one of the coldest winters in living memory. The next excursion to my vantage point turned out to be truly staggering. Virtually every able-bodied person on the reservation was readying himself or herself to hunt for yet more wood. With supreme self-assurance, borne from my latest surveillance, I duly informed the good people of Browning that records were likely to be broken over the next few months and that this coming winter was definitely gonna be right at the peak of the SHIVERING POLAR BEAR category.

My next Indian surveillance revealed no let up on the wood gathering; in fact I would say that virtually every able-bodied person in the reservation had been assigned to the task. That morning I really went to town at what turned out to be my last forecast for the station, although I did not realise that at the time. Folks, I said in my most solemn voice, we must all make sure that those home fires are kept burning big, bright and beautiful. I can't stress to you enough as to just how cold this winter is gonna be. Get them bunkers packed with coal; the oil tanks filled to the brim and the wood shed stacked to the rafters.

Later that day Henry Merryweather (honest), the station director, sent for me. Jack, he says in a most concerned tone, I know your record at the winter forecasting has been good in previous years, but the station has had hundreds of calls from anxious citizens regarding your insistence that this is likely to be the coldest winter on record, despite the fact that all other evidence points to the contrary. The mercury is still a good ten degrees above freezing and folks are worried that they're going over the top spending their hard earned dollars on buying fuel based purely on what you are telling 'em. Have I ever let you down boss I replied with more conviction than I actually felt? It was true that all meteorological indications suggested a sustained mild period and yet I couldn't believe that the Indians could get it so wrong.

Nevertheless I decided to play it safe and so the next morning instead of parking up at my usual vantage point, I carried straight on into the reservation itself. The camp was virtually deserted as just about every resident was elsewhere – yes you've guessed it – out gathering wood. This comforted me somewhat as I made for the Chief's home. The Chief lived in a roomy wood and chrome trailer and on this particularly balmy morning he was sat on the steps, a lonely figure in the still and silent camp.

After an exchange of the usual pleasantries, I carefully broached the subject regarding his nation's uncanny knack at weather forecasting. I massaged his ego whilst trying to extract the secret. His initial shield of caution was eventually lowered as he told me of the great store his people placed on such natural phenomena as the height of the beaver's dam; the work rate of the wild bees as they harvested the nectar from the autumn flowers and the time that the bears went into hibernation. However, he added with increasing smugness, as good as these signs are, we Blackfeet like to think we can also embrace the white man's technology and so this year for the first time we have been tuning in every morning to the weather forecast on KBWG – You know that guy Jack Clancy is bloody good. He gets it right every time and though the usual signs pointed towards a mild winter we know that good old Jack won't let us down – I just don't know how he does it!"

It was at this point that the first salty tear dropped from Jack's weary eye and splashed silently into his now warm beer ------------.

A Room With A View?

Steve and Pete had been placed in adjoining beds in the military wing of the local hospital. The pair had been inseparable friends since junior school and were more like brothers than just mere friends. They had played in the same Sunday league football team, worked at the same factory as fitters and drank in the same pubs. So close was their relationship that they had even courted and eventually married twin sisters, Sharon and Alice.

During the past decade or so the employment situation in their small provincial town had come to be somewhat unstable and it was therefore no great surprise when just a few months before their planned double wedding the unfortunate pair were made redundant. All efforts in seeking other work in the area were unsuccessful until that fateful day they stood outside the Army Recruiting Office. It appeared that of all the prospective employers in the town the military were the only organization offering the chance of a permanent position.

Initially the girls were none to happy when informed that their prospective husbands had signed up for a lengthy period of service but eventually came to accept that unless they wished to exist on benefits for the foreseeable future then it was after all a sound and practical decision. They were even more delighted when soon after the wedding bells had ceased to ring and their new 'hubbies' had completed their initial training, they were allocated to adjoining married quarters in a military camp not too far from their home town.

Just over a year after their nuptials, Steve and Pete were over the moon when their respective partners announced that they were to be fathers. It was while they were celebrating the fantastic news that the not entirely unexpected bombshell dropped. The unit in which they served was to be posted to Afghanistan to play their part in helping to restore law and order in a war that for far to long had ravaged the country. The girls were obviously concerned for the safety of their men folk but were sensible enough to know that as serving soldiers, such a posting was always possible. By now both Sharon and Alice were heavily pregnant with their first born as they put on their bravest faces and waved the boys off to do their bit for Queen and country as so many army wives had done over the preceding years....

The day as usual had been unmercifully hot and made even more unbearable with the heavy weight of their equipment and body armour. It had however been somewhat uneventful as Steve and Pete, along with their dozen or so comrades-in-arms patrolled the near deserted village on the edge of Helmund Province. The only inhabitants of this unholy and inhospitable community appeared to be the half-starved dogs that whined incessantly in their fruitless search for food. As Steve took that fateful step forward to pat one of the mangy creatures he heard the ominous click that all patrolling servicemen had been warned about. He had inadvertently triggered an explosive devise cunningly concealed in the dusty earth. He just had time to scream a warning to his comrades before the full force of the device caught him and his ever faithful pal Pete who as ever was by his side.....

By some miracle, both men survived although terribly injured by the explosion and for a time it had been touch and go. After many transfusions, bone settings and comatose weeks in the field hospital where they were patched up as well as the limited resources would allow, they were eventually repatriated to 'blighty' – The Afghan campaign for the brave duo was well and truly over!

Yet even now, though both critically injured, the lifelong friends could not be parted. Steve, who had taken the worst of the blast, could do nothing more than lie flat on his back as every movement for him was agony. Pete had fared slightly better and had been given the bed by the ward's only window where each afternoon he was allowed to sit up in his bed for an hour or so to help drain the fluid from his lungs. As the long painful days turned into weeks the pair gradually improved their physical condition and spent the seemingly endless hours reminiscing about their lives prior to that eventful day in that cursed country which had so nearly cost them their lives. They spoke of their time in school when Steve had nearly been caught having a crafty cigarette behind the bike sheds. They laughed at the time their football team turned a 3-goal half-time deficit into a 4-3 win with both of them getting on the score sheet. They chatted about their homes, their jobs, the places they had visited on holidays, their involvement in the military service, but most of all they talked lovingly of their wives and babies, two fine strapping lads apparently who they had yet to meet face to face.

At the times when Pete was allowed to sit up in his bed, he would pass the time by describing to his pal all the things he could see outside the window. Steve began to live for those periods where his lonely world would be broadened and enlivened by all the activity and colour of the real world outside. According to Pete's detailed commentaries, the window overlooked a beautifully tended park with a sparkling blue lake in the centre. Ducks, swans and all manner of other waterfowl swam on the clear waters while young children played happily along the fringes of the lake whilst the older ones sailed their model boats. He told of the young lovers walking arm in arm amidst immaculate beds containing blooms of every shape and colour and in the distance there was a spectacular view of the city skyline.

As Pete portrayed all these wonderful sights in exquisite detail, Steve would close his eyes and imagine the picturesque scenes as painted by his friend. One particularly warm afternoon, Pete described a military parade passing by. Although Steve could neither hear nor see the band - he could picture it in his mind's eye as Pete revealed its splendour with such accurate and descriptive words.

The days, weeks and months continued to pass. Steve's health improved beyond the doctors' wildest hopes, thanks in the main to Pete's remarkable daily commentaries. One morning, the nurse arrived to bring water for their daily ablutions only to discover Pete's lifeless body. He had lost the fight to overcome his many injuries and had died peacefully in his sleep. The young nurse was saddened and called the hospital attendants to take the body away. Steve was devastated by the loss of his friend. He himself was over the worst of his ordeal and as soon as it seemed appropriate, he asked if he could be moved next to the window so that he could see for himself the wonderful views that Pete had described so vividly. The nurse was happy to make the move and after making sure that he was settled and comfortable, she left him alone.

Slowly and painfully Steve propped himself up on one elbow to take his first look at the real world outside. He strained manfully and with much effort he eventually managed to raise his eyes above the window's edge and looked out from the bed so recently occupied by his best buddy and gazed in expectation at - a blank wall! Steve was naturally shocked and taken aback at the discovery. And asked the nurse what could have compelled Pete, who had described such wonderful things outside this window, to be so deceitful. The nurse, as gently as possible replied, "Perhaps he just wanted to encourage you."

Steve's mind was in turmoil. How could you know a person for most of your life only to discover that they were capable of such downright deception? However, the more he mulled it over the more he came to accept that the nurse's prognosis of wanting to encourage him was probably pretty accurate. Pete was that kind of guy - Caring to a fault. Steve decided to chat some more with the nurse. After all he had little else to do, and she was really quite pretty.

"You know the strange thing about it was the vivid way he described the imaginary scene," Steve said to the nurse as she sat at the end of his bed. "Don't get me wrong, he was a great guy but didn't have a lot of imagination. He will probably be walking round heaven now and describing it as 'interesting'. How could anyone with such a limited imagination describe a scene so vividly while staring at nothing more than a blank wall?"

"It's more remarkable than you think," replied the nurse. "As hard as he might have tried he couldn't even see the wall! As a result of his injuries he couldn't see anything at all. He was totally blind."

Never Doubt A Lady

There was little doubt that the house was haunted. Down through the years, ever since the initial tragedy had occurred, there had been sightings and yet the doubts and cynicism remained with the proclaimed visitations being dismissed by unbelievers as mere figments of an overactive imagination.

Charlotte had seen her on more than one occasion yet surprisingly she had never been frightened or alarmed in the presence of the ghostly figure. The apparition, far from being scary or threatening, exuded instead an aura of concerned sympathy that was at once apparent to those who were receptive to the spectral vibrations – and here the real mystery begins.

Legend had it that that the spectre only appeared to those who had recently lost loved ones and was destined to spend the rest of their earthly life alone, unable or unwilling to replace that, which had been so cruelly torn from them by that surest of all fates – death!

The foundation of the legend was rooted back in the 17th century, when the house had been in the possession of the Markham family. The Markham's were nobly born, albeit rather well down in the social scale of English aristocracy and had therefore considered themselves duty bound to support the royalist cause during the civil war. Sir Grenville Markham, the head of the household, had taken to himself a wife, Sarah, who was as radiant and pleasing a woman as any man could wish to marry. So great was his love and devotion for Sarah, coupled with an outrageous fear that one day he would lose her affection, that he had forced her to swear a terrible oath that forbade her from ever loving another man during her husband's lifetime – or if the fates decreed, even after his death.

Among Lady Sarah's many attributes was a great sense of loyalty and an unquestioning desire to please her husband in all things. It was therefore of no great surprise to her family and friends, when hearing of Sir Grenville's mortal wounds in a gallant though foolhardy action at Marston Moor, she declared that from that day no man would ever hold favour in her heart, even to her dying day. Lady Sarah was true and steadfast to her vow and so she passed from youthful beauty to her deathbed without the warmth and comfort of any other man.

The coming of death unfortunately, although realising her mortal remains to the grave, did not free her spirit from earthly bondage, for she was condemned to reveal herself in spectral form to all who were to suffer a similar loss as her own.

Charlotte and Clive had learned of the legend almost as soon as they had taken residence in the old house. However, they were not particularly affected by what they considered to be superstitious nonsense and had dismissed the possibility of a haunting as being most unlikely.

Clive worked for a large international oil company and his job took him to all the far-flung corners of the globe. Charlotte had entered into the marriage fully aware of the probabilities of many forced absences, but still it came hard when after the all to few interludes of happiness she was continually forced to lose him to the dangerous world of oil exploration...

Charlotte's first sighting of Lady Sarah occurred during one of her husband's enforced journeys abroad. It was soon after the Suez crisis and anxious to find other sources of oil, the company had sent Clive out to South America in the hope that commercial deposits of the 'black gold' could be found and exploited.

The sighting had puzzled rather than frightened Charlotte for knowing by then the supposed implication of such a visitation she knew that Clive was alive and well as she had received a letter from him only that morning – But still, the way the phantom had held her gaze with such an intense though pitiful stare had caused Charlotte some concern as it had contained within its depths the shared grieve that is unique between women who have lost loved ones in tragic circumstances.

The initial misgiving deepened to actual concern, as weeks passed without further correspondence from her loved one. The fears became groundless on the receipt of Clive's next letter. She read and re-read every paragraph and sentence, savouring each word, much as a scholar would on discovering a long lost Shakespearian manuscript. She knew that every comma, semicolon and full stop contained a vital message - That her love was alive.

The next encounter with Lady Sarah was therefore even more intriguing as the wraithlike spirit glided down the long staircase. Charlotte longed to inform her that her ghostly intuition had failed and that Clive was in fact alive and well, yet she could not help but be concerned at the deep sorrow she beheld in the ethereal eyes that had known over three centuries of sorrow and grief. Troubled thoughts invaded her erstwhile no-nonsense world – and she was afraid...

Rat-a-tat-tat! The insistent rap of the knocker brought her rudely from her reverie and she hurried to answer its demanding call. Somehow she knew it would be a telegram. The outline of the telegraph boy's uniform was

just about discernable through the translucent glass of the front door as she opened it with trembling hands.
"Any reply ma'am," chirped the youthful cockney voice as Charlotte attempted to bring the bold black type into focus.
PARTY MISSING – STOP – BELIEVED LOST IN FLOODS – STOP – EMPTY BOAT FOUND – STOP – FEAR NO SURVIVORS – STOP:
Stop – Stop; the word echoed and re-echoed through her tormented mind. The one word that made any real sense in that awful moment. The one command that a tormented soul like hers could comprehend – for now would life not stop for her also? At that awful moment she truly believed that there was no reason for existence to continue without Clive.
The initial shock gradually abated although she spent many miserable and tearful hours alone in her locked and shuttered room. Rational thought eventually overcame an erstwhile jumble of crazy emotions, many inevitably centred on Lady Sarah. She had known the truth after all. It had been foolish of Charlotte to deny or doubt the power of unknown supernatural forces.
The days lengthened to weeks and though the pain of losing such a dear love had diluted somewhat, Charlotte still felt that part of her was also missing. Her only succour during those dark days and endless nights had been the more frequent visits from Lady Sarah. She came now as a consoling figure, her eyes full of understanding and compassion and though no words were uttered, her very presence had been an immense comfort.

Charlotte finally came to a decision. She knew she must not spend the rest of her life mourning her loss, enshrined in an aura of self-pity with her only companion a ghost, albeit one who had brought some small measure of relief. She had put the house up for sale and resolved herself in returning to the world of commercial art, a world she had willingly forsaken to take up the role of Clive's full time wife. Lady Sarah, as if anticipating the impending departure, had been a more frequent visitor. Her every presence reminding Charlotte that she was alone and unloved and by remaining here she would be fated to continue in that unfulfilled state...

By sheer coincidence it was the same telegraph boy who delivered the second telegram.

DARLING – STOP – THOROUGHLY SOAKED BUT ALIVE AND WELL – STOP – ARRIVE HEATHROW MONDAY – STOP – LOVE, CLIVE.

Charlotte hugged and kissed the startled youth. Her joy knew no bounds. She had been reborn once more. No longer was she destined to live a life of solitude – Clive was alive!

With sudden awareness, Charlotte's thoughts were directed towards her erstwhile comforter.

"She was wrong," she whispered elatedly to herself. "For once she really got it wrong." Charlotte hurried inside. She had this crazy notion of reading the telegram out loud to Lady Sarah and crown the reading with a triumphant, "You were wrong! You were oh so wrong. He is alive and I will see him again."

Strangely enough, the ghostly figure of Lady Sarah was hovering, motionless at the foot of the sweeping

staircase; her eyes were steady and unblinking, still full of sadness and pity as she listened to the contents of that blessed telegram. The melancholic pose so filled Charlotte with amusement that she threw back her head and laughed loud and long.
"Why won't you admit you were wrong this time?" yelled a now exuberant Charlotte. "Even you cannot ignore the proof that Clive lives." Defiantly she shook the now crumpled telegram at Lady Sarah, seeking some response from the shadowy figure – but Lady Sara remained impassive...

The pilot had no chance of controlling the wildly veering plane. It had almost reached take off speed on the main runway of Caracus airport, when, as if from nowhere, the lone woman with the sad eyes appeared directly in his path. His vain attempts to evade the shadowy figure had placed undue stress on the undercarriage, which collapsed, causing the huge craft to turn completely over and career like some stricken giant bird into the surrounding bush...
The rescue team reported that there were no survivors!

The Bridge

"Sachin!" the man in the sweat stained khaki called for the third time. "Sachin, you lazy good for nothing black faced heathen, where the hell have you got to?" The fierce tropical sun blazed down with relentless inevitability. Its heat so intense that he felt the victim of some ghastly cosmic plot, hatched with the sole Intention of fusing his body and the red earth together as one. Just standing there was proving an effort; to shout in apparent

futility bordered on a Herculean task not to be undertaken lightly.
Tom Roberts though was in need of help. A month's confinement in the coastal military hospital after a rather nasty bout of enteric fever had left him in no mood for a somewhat enforced return to his unit, which was located in a mosquito infested inferno, named by someone with a peculiar sense of humour, the Plain of serenity.
The day had started wrong for Roberts. He'd slopped scalding tea on his hand and had ruefully philosophised that heat was about the only comparative virtue that the hospital 'brew' shared with the 'civvy' counterpart. This initial act of misfortune had resulted in a less than steady hold on his razor, which had resulted in two bad 'nicks' that had done nothing for his appearance or his humour and as if to round off his disastrous morning, all he saw of his official transport back to the camp was the rear end of an army ambulance disappearing round the hospital block in a cloud of dust and a grinding of unmeshed gears.
Dame Fortune finally relented by removing at least one of the fated dice that he had been rolling that morning when he managed to beg a lift from a transporter that would be passing within 3 miles of the camp – and it was here that he now found himself, dumped unceremoniously to fathom out his next move.
Normally this would have presented few difficulties as this intersection of roads was a well used dropping off place for military personnel travelling to Camp Serenity and as such was normally frequented by native boys offering portaging services for the strange sahibs who would rather pay than carry their own luggage. Unfortunately

those rather fickle dice had decreed the spot deserted – and poor Tom found himself quite alone.

The noonday sun seemed to burn with a renewed ferocity as he stood there taking in huge gulps of scorched air that seared his lungs with its unpalatable taste. His rounded shoulders rose and fell with the strain and beads of sweat stood out on his craggy features like a myriad of precious stones, each one catching the glare of the sun and diffusing the light which half-blinded him and only served to add to his general discomfort.

He shook his head, disturbing the droplets that showered to the parched earth where they were immediately soaked up – the ground showing no signs as to where they had fallen. His lungs rasped once more as he drew on the fetid air, preparing for the final attempt to summon Sachin from whatever secret place he had chosen to hide in. Tom was convinced he was within earshot but with typical native indifference he was choosing to ignore the calls until it suited him to appear.

Tom contemplated the situation with a forced detachment. On reflection it wasn't Sachin's style to hide if there was a profit to be gained, nor would he normally flinch from tasks that his peers would shun. In fact of all the 'char wallas' and 'bhistis' that had descended on the camp during its construction, Sachin had earned a sort of grudging respect for his industrious ways from even the most seasoned in the ranks. Most days he could be found, like a modern day 'Gunga DIn', squatting on the dusty earth, waiting to offer his services for the scantiest of rewards.

Sachin's appearance belied his actual physical capabilities. Standing little over five feet tall with the sunken chest and rickets scarred knees, so typical of poor diet, disease and other privations that marked many of the local populace indicated little of the dynamic forces that motivated the seemingly inferior frame into tasks avoided by men of lesser breed. His ungainly arms ridiculed the symmetry of the normal limb, being at once unusually long and slender but with a suppleness that allowed him to perform the most astonishing feats with a nonchalant ease and an air of indifference and modesty still found in less sophisticated cultures.

The philosophic bargain that Sachin had struck with his maker was epitomised in his face. Resigned to an existence of perpetual toil and struggle, the small wizened features prematurely aged by fierce sunlight and the inevitable dust were set in a permanent grin that never faltered no matter what the circumstances. A grin so steadfastly maintained that it appeared to be carved on his face by some mischievous sculptor and neither beatings nor curses had been known to diminish its intensity.

His jet-black hair was plastered western fashion to his scalp by a curious mixture of palm oil and sweat that gave off an odour just on the offensive side of unusual. However, this strange hair preparation added a sheen and lustre to his crowning glory that obviously attracted certain ladies of his village.

Unfortunately for Tom Roberts though, neither a flash of the impish grin or the slightest whiff of native hair oil was apparent to relieve him of the now physical strain he was suffering from shouldering his seemingly expanding kitbag.

"Damn his dirty brown hide." The curse slipped from between Tom's clenched teeth as he sought an easier place on his back for the gear that from time immemorial the universal soldier had been compelled to carry with him at all times. It appeared now that the only way he was destined to reach camp that day with his burden was by acting as his own porter.

He trudged resignedly towards the smudge on the horizon that was Camp Serenity. His feet shuffled wearily through the red dust, throwing up little swirls and eddies of the stuff that clung to his boots, masking the familiar black under a coating of crimson.

The walk gave him time to collect his thoughts and as each step took him painfully towards his objective, the northern phlegmatic attitudes nurtured on hard times and disappointments transcended the baser feelings and his erstwhile rage dwindled to the comparative passion of mere annoyance. He contemplated his immediate future and considered what life had in store for him during the three months remaining of his present tour of duty. He resigned himself to spending it in the unending routine of military life, where the high spot of the week was Saturday night in the 'Naafi', a half-dozen or so bottles of tepid beer and good old Barney the Les Dawson of the 2nd battalion, belting out the 'golden oldies' of yesteryear with all the enthusiasm and verve of a demolition worker in full cry.

As Tom reached the foot of a small rise, his reveries were disturbed by an unfamiliar sound. Curiosity lent strength to his weary limbs and he hurried to the crest of the hill. Before him lay a panoramic view of the camp. It was quite a large set up really considering its apparent strategic unimportance, with the rows of regularly positioned huts. Like well drilled ranks of infantry, set out in some vast war game – all standing to attention and waiting for a command to advance.

This semblance of military order was marred only by the meandering of a wide river that threaded its way through the camp in somewhat haphazard fashion. But even in the presence of Mother Nature military precision was not to be denied and so it served the purpose of neatly bisecting the camp into officers and NCOs quarters on the west bank and other ranks on the east.

It was this usual turgid flow of cocoa like composition that was responsible for the unusual sound. Prolonged rainstorms in the hills to the north had turned the once passive river into a muddy brown torrent. The normal swirl and soft lap of the water had changed its tune to a bass roar as raging waters tumbled along its course as if pursued by unseen tormentors.

Tom gazed on the alien scene for many minutes. It seemed that here he was, surrounded as far as the eye could see by acres of sterile land which rarely felt the kiss of soft summer rain; never felt the birth pangs of tender shoots breaking through its dusty surface; barren – because this very source of life had denied its touch, apart from the narrow band which now roared relentlessly on to discharge into a salty grave in some far off sea.

The seed of life was undoubtedly present in abundance, yet here he stood, lone witness to countless gallons of the

precious stuff, which in this mad moment of nature gone awry was running literally to waste. Only the riverbank would profit from the floodtide and already he ascertained prolific growth of desert blooms that parenthesised the watercourse.
Tom trudged down the sandy rise and heard the hiss and roar of the tumultuous water flow grow to a deafening crescendo with every step he took. He stopped a few feet from the bank, apprehensive at venturing further as the force of the river's passage shook the earth around him with its awesome power.
As Tom took in the grim scene before him he realized that he was on the wrong side of the torrent and that his destination lay on the opposite bank. This in itself presented no particular problem as not one but two bridges spanned the river, giving the traveller a choice of routes.
The two bridges were classics of contrast; the old native bridge constructed with varying sections of bamboo with the more mature growths acting as piles and supports while the younger branches formed the walkway and handrails. The construction was held together with bark strips and liana vines and had stood for many years, serving the needs of the native populace most effectively. The new bridge in comparison was a model of military engineering. Reinforced concrete piles had been driven through the sandy earth until they rested on bedrock some twenty or more feet down. Smooth metal columns rose out of the water at precise intervals, their very shape suggesting a strength and stability that would undoubtedly pass the test of time. The columns were

criss-crossed by a tracery of girder work that gave the bridge a support potential many tons in excess of its heaviest loads.

It was the crude native bridge though which carried the volume of pedestrian traffic and the reason for this choice was easy to see. The long dead builders had applied their simple native logic to the business of crossing the river. They had selected the narrowest point and having no knowledge of geology, hydraulics or other construction sciences had but one criteria – locate the narrowest point and build your bridge.

By coincidence, the old bridge linked both sides of the camp almost dead centre whilst the monumentally engineered military bridge was some 300 metres upstream, built of course on the firmest foundations the army engineers could find. It was not surprising therefore that the official crossing place was something of a white elephant, shunned by all except for vehicular traffic. The army brass hats of course were dismayed when they realized that many pounds of taxpayer's money had been spent on a construction used perhaps three or four times a day. In a vain attempt to redress the situation they had condemned the old bridge as unsafe and had ordered all crossings of the river to be made via the new bridge. Not surprisingly the edict was never strictly enforced and even the C.O. paid only lip service to it.

As it happened, Tom's approach to the camp had carried him to a point where the old native bridge was nearest. He saw it now, looming out of the spray, not thirty metres away with the rushing waters no more than inches away from the actual walkway. In the far distance the military

bridge stood as firm and imposing as ever, the watery spate parted by the immovable columns seemed to sense the futility of trying to topple the structure and so rushed on, hoping to wreak havoc among less sturdy targets.
Tom had reached the old bridge, now shaking ominously as the unforgiving waters rushed by; thirty or forty strides would he knew carry him to the safety of the other bank – He made up his mind quickly. Exhausted by the trials and tribulations of the day he was determined to reach his billet and rest his weary body by taking the shortest route possible.
He had taken his first tentative step onto the bridge when, out of the corner of his eye, he saw that for which he had been searching this long weary hour. It was Sachin, standing some fifty or so metres upstream, grinning as only he could like some demented caricature out of a comic book.
Tom's urgent intent on reaching his billet vanished as he behold the one person he believed most responsible for his present debilitated condition. He stepped off the bridge and strode purposefully towards his perceived tormentor.
"Sachin – where the blazes have you been hiding?" he yelled as he approached the spindly figure whose grin now appeared to be mocking him. Instead of an answer Sachin shuffled away and as hard as Tom tried he could not close the distance between them.
Sachin walked on, turning once to wave in the direction of his pursuer as if beckoning him to follow. Tom needed no encouragement and the gesture did nothing to placate the rage smouldering in his breast. A deep bass rumbling

that was audible even above the water's roar interrupted his outraged indignation. He turned to see the old bridge shuddering ominously like some stricken beast. The whole structure stood poised for what seemed an eternity – then with a sickening low grind that grew to a terrible crescendo, the bridge disintegrated before the awesome power of the river and in an instance – was gone. All that remained was the odd spar of bamboo that rose to the surface of the maelstrom, only to be sucked under once more and reduced to nothing more that foot long splinters, which was all that was ever found of the bridge. The colour drained from Tom's face as he realized the awful fate he would have suffered if he had not been diverted from crossing the old bridge by his sighting of Sachin. The full implication finally dawned on his numbed senses. Without realizing it Sachin had undoubtedly saved his life. He thought of all the minor mishaps of the day and laughed with relief to think of the importance he had attached to them. He knew that now he must catch up with Sachin to heap on him the rewards so justly if somewhat fortuitously earned.

Sachin had now crossed the seemingly unmoveable military bridge and was now hurrying towards the camp. Tom raced after him, determined to catch him as soon as possible. He crossed the bridge and hurried off in the direction of the camp. As he approached the nearest huts he saw Sachin facing him, that ubiquitous grin now so pronounced appeared to split his face into two distinct halfs.

"Sachin – you old son of a gun, stand still for a minute can't you?" Sachin's only response was to lift his long

skinny arm in a gesture of farewell before walking swiftly round the side of the nearest hut. Tom quickened his pace and ran towards the hut. As he rounded the corner he narrowly avoided collision with one of his army comrades.
"Steady on there Tom, you're going to mow somebody down moving at that pace – what's the big hurry anyway?"
"Sachin I'm trying to catch up with Sachin," Tom replied breathlessly. There was a strained silence as the soldier eyed Tom quizzically.
"Well old boy you'll have to run a damn sight faster than that to catch him. He was one of the poor blighters that caught that blasted enteric fever. He died day before yesterday – They buried him this morning."

THE LAST BUS

He had checked his clothes carefully, making sure there was no visible evidence of blood splatter. If only the stupid kid had handed over the contents of the till instead of trying to act the hero. He hadn't intended to hit him quite as hard with the charity tin but it was nearly Christmas and the generous customers of the little isolated garage had obviously been feeling more benevolent than usual, as it was almost full of assorted coinage and must have weighed a good kilo or more.

Wayne was sink estate toughened and not many sights had scared him over the last thirty-odd years, but even he had shuddered at the gory sight of the youth's caved in skull; his life's blood pulsing from the horrific wound, staining the white of his 'Spurs football shirt a bright crimson. However, the spectacle had conjured no more than a fleeting pang of regret in Wayne's cold heart as he had wrested the blood soaked notes from the young man's hand before fleeing into a swirling grey mist that added to the darkness of the night...

As he trudged down the silent and desolate country road, Wayne mused over the circumstances that had led him into the unfamiliar territory of the Home Counties. He was currently serving a 30-year sentence as society's punishment for a number of heinous atrocities committed over a near lifetime of criminal activity in and around the northern town where he had been born and raised.

His speciality had been breaking into churches or other religious institutions and stealing anything that he could sell to feed his insatiable drug habit. It had been unfortunate that his last raid had taken place in a small convent chapel. It certainly proved more than unfortunate for the priest and two sisters who had confronted him as he attempted to flee with a large and ornate brass candlestick. The local constabulary forces had found him in his grimy tenement apartment nonchalantly removing the last traces of blood and matted hair from the heavy base of the candlestick, which he had used to batter the life from the three saintly people who had attempted to thwart his unholy plundering.

On passing sentence, the judge had decreed that because of the monstrous scale of this and previous vile criminal acts and his numerous escape attempts from lower category prisons, that he be incarcerated in Belmarsh, the countries top high security prison in the capital. No doubt if the vehicle transporting him there had reached its destination, Wayne would undoubtedly have found escape nigh on impossible – But it hadn't.

Wayne was not the only prisoner being transported that day and he found himself sharing the high-tech' conveyance with a notorious and well-connected drug baron. It was about 30 miles from Belmarsh in the heart of the Hertfordshire countryside when the vehicle came to a juddering halt. Then came the sound of gunshots and moments later the armoured rear door was prised open to reveal a number of armed and hooded men who gestured for the two manacled prisoners to leave the van quickly.

Unable to fully grasp at first what was happening, Wayne stood submissively while the handcuffs were removed. Once freed of his restraints he was totally ignored whilst his erstwhile criminal companion was escorted to a waiting high-powered limousine. The unconscious guards were bundled unceremoniously into the back of the security vehicle before it was sent plunging down the steep embankment that flanked the road. Whatever their fate was destined to be, Wayne neither knew or cared. The important thing was that he was free. Two minutes later he found himself totally alone, the escape car now nothing more than a dot in the distance – It was then in the gathering gloom that he had spotted the lights of the little rural garage…

That disastrous events that had taken place in the garage already seemed to be half a lifetime away as he trudged wearily along the road. Not a vehicle of any description had passed him since he had gained his freedom and the yellowy grey mist blotted out any geographical features that may have helped to determine just where he was or where he was heading.

He had just about given up hope of a vehicle passing when in the distance he thought he heard the throaty roar of a lorry or large van – And then, approaching him from the direction in which he had just walked, he saw the distinctive lights of – A double-decker bus! As it drew nearer he saw the dim light of the destination plate – 'HAYES'. Though geography was not his strong point the name did sound a little familiar. Maybe I can find a cheap hotel there and clean myself up a bit, he thought to himself. Now if I can only get it to stop.

Thankfully, and with a squeal of ancient brakes, it did stop. He was somewhat surprised to find that the bus was a very old model with access being at the rear. There appeared to be quite a few souls on the lower deck and so Wayne decided he would probably find it quieter on the upper deck – and it was. There were but six other passengers up here, all seated to the front of the bus. Two females, who from their hooded attire appeared to be nuns, a man, who with his prominent 'dog-collar' was obviously a priest of some kind, a couple of guys in uniforms of some description and a rather skinny youth wearing a dark hooded top and a somewhat grubby red football shirt. Wayne slid as inconspicuously as he could into a rear seat and fished in his pocket for his bus fare.

The strains of the old Elvis favourite 'You're the Devil in Disguise' came from the stairwell, hummed by the chirpy conductor as he made his way to the upper deck. "Anymore fares please," he called loudly. Wayne offered up a grubby bloodstained note and said,

"Single please mate, all the way."

"That's the only fare we do on this 'ere bus mister. We don't do returns, and aint you got anything smaller?" he replied eyeing the stained note with undisguised suspicion.

"Keep the change," Wayne responded. "Plenty more where that came from," he continued with a wicked grin.

"I'll give you a couple of coins for the ferry then. You don't want to be stuck on the wrong side of the river now do you?" Wayne looked a little taken aback. He hadn't reckoned on catching a ferry to get to Hayes. "How long before we get there," inquired Wayne of the conductor? "And any cheap lodgings where I can get my head down for a while?"

"Now just let me check on that," smiled the conductor as he pulled a rather imposing notebook from his pocket. "Looks like you're the last pick-up tonight Wayne old son and it's pretty much all downhill from here. Reckon about two hours or so will find us at our final destination. As for getting your head down, well that's not likely to happen. But not to worry, the accommodation may not be wholly to your liking but at least it's warm and free," he added with a wicked grin.

A couple of things struck Wayne. How can he be so certain that I'm the last passenger as surely there will be more bus stops between here and Hayes? But more concernedly, how the blazes did he know my name? Lucky guess I reckon, he mused to himself.
"Are these other passengers going all the way as well?" he asked. "Well they aint exactly passengers as such Wayne," responded the conductor. "More like – er – um – helpers for you; ye that's what they are – helpers." "I don't need help from a couple of penguins, a sky pilot and a hoodie," replied Wayne vehemently. "Well let's say persuaders then – Ye I reckon that's closer to the mark – persuaders."

Wayne gave the conductor a disdainful look before settling further in his seat. The guy was certainly right about going downhill. He reckoned that this was just about the steepest road he'd travelled and as it was also getting decidedly warmer, Wayne's eyelids drooped...

With a squeal of those ancient brakes the rickety bus came to a shuddering halt. Wayne was awakened from his uneasy slumber and found himself being borne aloft by six pairs of cold white hands belonging to a couple of nuns, a priest, two prison warders and a 'hoodie' in a bloodstained 'Spurs football shirt.
As he was flung screaming into the fiery pit, Wayne caught one last sight of the damned bus and the destination plate he had struggled to read that first time when it had emerged ghostlike from the mist. He had misread it by one letter. It wasn't bound for 'HΛYES' after all. As hellish as some people may find this urban development, it could never hope to compete with the unholy destination that now shone out so distinctly –

'HADES'.

VENI, VIDI not so VICI

It was certainly not a day that Julius would have chosen to go walking in the wilds of Northumberland. Any lone trek would have been considered imprudent in the middle of a harsh English winter but up on this bleak inhospitable escarpment, in the shadow of Hadrian's Wall, with a stiffening breeze threatening to escalate to gale proportions and sombre snow clouds thickening it was positively reckless.

But if not today there would be no further opportunity for Julius to realize a childhood dream. It was the last chance for him to walk along this splendid example of

Roman engineering that stretched the breadth of the country. Since he had first seen the atmospheric photograph of the magnificent structure in his school textbook, he had vowed that one day he would walk at least a section of the wall. Business had been the primary reason for him to be so far from the bright lights of London. However, it had been concluded successfully and tomorrow he would return to base with a full order book and the bonus that was sure to ensue would certainly help to reduce his now familiar post Christmas overdraft.

In anticipation of realizing his childhood ambition, Julius had packed some basic walking equipment and as he fought against the growing force of the wind he was certainly glad of the bright red walking jacket, his fleece lined headgear, a stout pair of boots and his trusty walking poles. It came as no great surprise when the first wind born snow crystals stung his cheeks. A more prudent individual would have called it a day and retraced their steps back to civilization but Julius was made of sterner stuff. He had planned to at least reach the first mile-castle along the wall and was relieved to make out through the gathering gloom the brooding outline of his objective.

Although this particular fort was in partial ruins, there was at least three of the four walls standing and even a goodly portion of the roof. As the storm was now growing in its ferocity, Julius decided to seek refuge in the rude but welcome shelter. He hunkered down as far into the corner of the ruin as he could, determined to ride out the worst of the tempest before returning to the comfort of his little B & B....

Julius came to with a start. Loud footsteps had awoken him from his unintended slumber and a shaft of moonlight now revealed the architect of those footfalls. He gazed up at the impressive figure that towered above him who was clad in the uniform of a Roman soldier. He rubbed his eyes and refocused, finding it difficult to accept the unusual sight before him. He suddenly recalled where he was and assumed that he was witnessing some sort of historical enactment of the Roman occupation in this part of the world.

"Come Julius," ordered the figure standing before him. "It's your turn for sentry duty with Marcus. We don't want those blasted Picts sneaking up on us again. Look lively man, you seem to be in some sort of dream." Julius came to his feet in a daze. The command made to him was in Latin; the scary part was that he understood every word. It became even scarier when he replied in the same tongue, "Where in Jupiter's name am I?"

"Silence you great blundering oaf. You dare to question the command of your centurion? I could have you flogged for that. Straighten your cloak and helmet; pick up your shield and spear and get out there before I put you on half-rations." Julius wondered what on earth this jumped up would be soldier was talking about until he paid closer attention to his own apparel. Around his shoulders there was indeed a poor quality and roughly woven red cloak where his expensive walking jacket had been. His fleece-lined hat was now a burnished metal helmet. One walking pole had somehow or other been transformed into a smooth-shafted spear, the other into a stout leather faced shield emblazoned with garish symbols. His mind raced uncontrollably as he tried to make sense of the bizarre situation. Was he still dreaming? The unaccustomed weight of the helmet on his head convinced him he was not. Was someone playing a huge practical joke on him then? As he glanced around at the now intact fortress and the dozen or so figures clad in similar attire to his own and on through the open doorway at the sight of a pristine wall with every stone looking as if it had been freshly laid, Julius realized that this was not the case.

Somehow or other he had been transported to the Roman occupied Britain of the 3rd Century AD and equally mystifying was the transformation of his 21st Century clothing into the military dress of the period. Even more perplexing was his immediate understanding of the language, which up to today had been limited to such universal phrases as 'Quo Vadis', 'Vox Populi and 'Veni Vidi Vici'. It was then it dawned on him. An avid science fiction fan he realized that somehow he had slipped through a fault in the space/time continuum. This combined with his sincere belief in human reincarnation went someway to explaining his current predicament.

A hard blow across his shoulder from the flat of a sword delivered by the centurion shook him out of his reverie. "If your not out on that wall before I count up to five then may Hercules protect you..... Unos, Duo Tres...." With a clatter of spear against shield, Julius dashed to join his fellow soldier on that seemingly impenetrable stone barrier.

Marcus was a chatterbox. As they slowly patrolled the wall he spoke of the latest news from home concerning the upstart Jew who had been crucified some two centuries earlier and was now being proclaimed as a God in some quarters. He regaled his reluctant companion with tales of his youth by the sunny shores of the Mediterranean. He spoke of his love of fine Etruscan wine, the thrill of watching gladiatorial combat and his numerous amorous conquests among the many slaves on his father's estate in Tuscany. He also spoke despondently of the grim and austere life he had been forced to lead since joining the army, an act apparently forced upon him by a despairing father in an effort to instil some Roman discipline in his wayward son, having lost patience with his decadent and debauched life style. Julius, not wanting to appear rude, nodded and agreed at appropriate intervals during his new companion's reminisces, while all the time trying to figure out as to how he could relocate the flaw in the space/time continuum fabric and return to his own less turbulent times. He deduced that the only way he was likely to achieve this end would be to exit the fort at the exact point where he had entered it.

At last the tour of sentry duty came to an end and Julius hurried back inside the somewhat cramped fortress determined to locate the space/time fault and return to his own era as soon as possible. It had been exciting while it lasted and he had certainly learned more about everyday Romans and their lives than he would ever have gleaned from any textbook. However there was only so much of Marcus's incessant chattering that he could take - and also that body armour weighed a ton and he was not sure just what he would have done if he had actually come face to face with an angry Pict. He had reasoned that the fault must be at one of the four doorways leading into the fort – but which one? He walked through three to no avail and was beginning to despair. At the fourth he thought he detected a faint shimmering blue light and his expectations rose. He strode boldly through it – and into a stygian blackness that totally overcame his consciousness...

With his head swimming wildly, Julius eventually recovered his senses to find himself on a vast treeless plain under a purple sky. There was no sign of a fortress; no trace of a wall and yet the distant hills appeared vaguely familiar. His cloak and armour had disappeared and he found himself clad in crudely fashioned animal hides. In his hand he carried a roughly hewn wooden club that was almost as large as him. In the near distance he thought he saw a flock of sheep grazing which comforted him somewhat. He shielded his eyes from the glare of a sun that was larger and hotter than he could ever remember and gazed at the flock, which were now heading purposefully in his direction. It was with a sense of horror that he realized that the godless creatures now approaching him at speed were not sheep or cows or any animal from the world that he was familiar with – they were sabre-tooth tigers – and they were hungry!

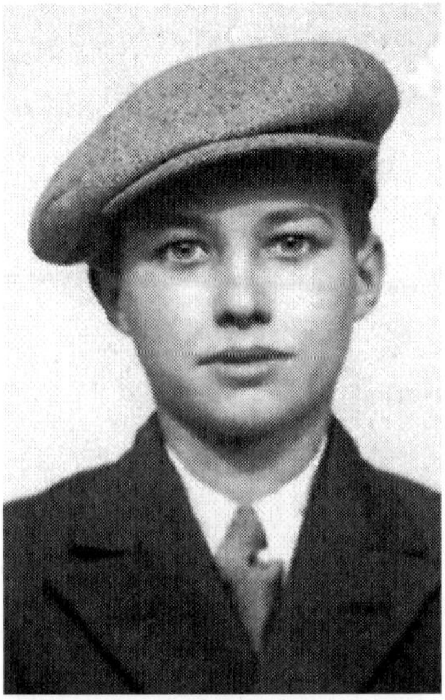

THE UNLIKELY HERO

Eli Hardcastle was one of humanity's nondescripts. At five foot two inches tall (or should that be short) and eight stone wet through, he would not have been noticeable even among a multitude of fellow nondescripts. His school life had been uneventful and being far from academic he had left with little or nothing to show for his endeavours, which in the late '30s, meant that his career choices were severely limited, particularly in the small northern industrial town of Crudington.

Fortunately for Eli, 'Grimley's', the local iron foundry always seemed to have vacancies for 'daft lads', as this was what Eli was adjudged to be by his peers and of course anyone who chose to spend nine hours a day in a dust laden atmosphere that you could cut with a knife could hardly be classified as anything else but 'daft'.

However, and despite his many shortcomings, Eli was a grafter and he eventually won the grudging respect of the foreman, who promoted him to Head Labourer. As promotions go, this one amounted to little, other than passing on the foreman's orders to three lads that were dafter than him. Nevertheless if they had placed a crown on his head and a sceptre in his hand he couldn't have been more proud - and it also gave him two bob extra in his weekly pay packet.

For the first dozen years or so of his working life he had lived with his beloved pigeons and devoted mum Lily, who had been a widow since Eli had been little more than a babe in arms. Early widowhood had been hard for Lily but had become much easier when her only child had started work and was able to supplement her meagre pension. She was also blessed by the fact that she had been able to buy their humble terraced cottage at 5 Ingot Street, thanks to the £250 she had received by way of compensation when her husband had so tragically fallen into a vat of molten metal at Grimley's. The purchase however turned out to be something of a mixed blessing - particularly for Eli...

Further down the somewhat grimy street at number 13 lived another widow woman called Bertha Winterbottom and her son Billy, who was of similar age to Eli. Bertha was not particularly popular with her neighbours due to her sharp tongue and the light-fingered activities of her feckless offspring, who had never held a job down for more than a couple of weeks. Bertha was shrewd and a cunning opportunist and when poor Lily sadly passed away, she spied her chance.

On the day after the funeral, Eli could be found wandering the mean streets of Crudington like a lost soul. Bertha, who had never been known to do a good turn for anyone in her life, caught him as he passed her door. "Hey up Eli. Come on in lad and have a bite to eat with Billy and me," she entreated him with mock sympathy. Eli was grateful, and besides, despite all her many and numerous faults, her cooking was almost as good as his late mum's. Well one thing led to another and within six months, despite the age difference, Bertha found herself with a ring on her finger and herself and Billy securely settled in at No 5...

"Them pigeons will 'av to go," ordered Bertha from the kitchen. "They're playing havoc with our Billy's asthma," she continued brusquely as she prepared dinner for the men in her life (steak and chips for Billy, beans and chips for Eli). He was about to respond by reminding her that a 20 pack of Woodbines a day, most of them scrounged from him, was probably the main reason for Billy's medical condition - but wisely thought better of it. After a disastrous honeymoon (a wet week-end in Blackpool), things went from bad to infinitely worse. She ruled him with a rod of iron, treated him like a slave and the only time her face displayed any emotion other than the almost permanent grimace of contempt was when he handed over his wage packet, unopened of course, every Friday night.

However, this latest bombshell regarding his beloved pigeons was just about the last straw. He could not imagine life without them and so, driven by desperation, he played the one card that he hoped would probably help change her mind - her love of shoes. Eli promised to get himself another job that would allow her to fulfil her passion for buying shoes, despite the fact that the cramped little house was already full of her size 7's.

With seemingly great reluctance she accepted the offer, even though it meant that Eli would be working more than fourteen hours a day. There had been one proviso to her acceptance and that was that he should build a proper loft for the 'flying rats' as she called them. Eli readily agreed and knew that he had enough in his 'secret' bank account to meet the cost of the materials required.

It was something of a coincidence that the part time job he had secured as a janitor should be at the very bank where he held his modest savings. This pleased him no end as in his simple mind he believed that the position allowed him to keep an eye on his money and he whistled a happy tune as he daily and diligently swept the ornate tiled floor of Boozy & Baggots First National Bank.

He had been there about six months when the attempted robbery took place. Eli as usual was cheerfully pushing his broom near the front entrance when the stout oak-panelled doors suddenly burst open and in strode two masked men, one brandishing a wicked looking club, the other what appeared to be a sawn-off shotgun. Now Eli had spent the whole of his humdrum life as a passive member of the human race and had never even raised his voice, never mind his fist to anyone, but this was different. Here were two villains intent on stealing his hard earned savings, to fritter away on beer and loose women, just at the time when he was planning a withdrawal to purchase the materials for his new pigeon loft - Well! He just wasn't having it.

With a deft flick of his wrist he brought the broom handle down hard on the head of the club-wielding robber and before his startled companion in crime could react he had sent the shotgun spinning from his hand. He brandished that ordinary broom like a rapier and with the apparent combined skills of D'artagnan, Cyrano DeBergerac and Errol Flynn all rolled into one he then felled the villain with a vicious upstroke to his unprotected chin...

The much-relieved bank had suitably rewarded Eli with an illuminated address relating his heroic actions and fifty guineas, which promptly found its way into Bertha's copious handbag. The red mist that had descended on Eli that eventful day had dissolved as quickly as it had appeared and he was back to his old submissive self, yet buoyed with the prospects of building the new pigeon loft. The materials were to be delivered that very day.

The award event had ended pleasantly enough with a ham salad and sandwich tea in the boardroom of the bank, spoilt only by Bertha hissing into Eli's ear that the reward had been derisory and that he should have received more. They finally departed but only after Bertha met the disapproving stare of the bank manager as she nonchalantly stuffed left over sandwiches into her bulging handbag.

As they neared the rear gate of their modest little house, a pall of smoke rising from the small backyard met them. Eli rushed forward into the yard where he was met

by the sight of Billy burning the newly delivered timber, meant for the loft construction.
"I thought it was just a load of old rubbish," he offered as a feeble excuse as the final pristine pine plank blackened in the heat of the fire - It was at that point that the aforesaid red mist descended on Eli once more...

It was the following morning when Eli was led to the waiting 'Black Maria' by members of the local constabulary. The fire was still smouldering but what really caught the eye were the two charred bodies on either side of what had now become a funeral pyre. One was of a rather scruffy and obese male whose mouth was stuffed by numerous packets of Wild Woodbines; the other was that of a stout middle-aged woman with just the heel of a black patent leather shoe protruding from between her thin blue lips...

Later that morning the postman delivered two letters to No 5, both bearing the Crudington town crest. One was a further congratulatory letter from the mayor regarding Eli's recent heroics; The other was from the planning department which stated quite simply, ***'The Planning Department of the borough of Crudington have viewed the plans submitted and regrets that permission to build a pigeon loft at 5 Ingot Street has been refused'*** - C'est la vie!

They Also Serve

"His actions were above and beyond the call of duty..." The Colonel was now in full flow as he extolled the virtues of the small but sturdy figure that stood at ease before him. *"Ignoring the bullets and shells that exploded about him,"* continued the smartly dressed officer, *"He made it with that vital message to the advance position that saved the lives of so many of his gallant comrades."*

Scottie was not the brightest spark in the ranks and much of what was been said regarding his gallant actions was certainly going over his black tousled head. He couldn't really understand what all the fuss was about. Hadn't he just been doing what all cocky Caledonians were

renowned for, looking for a scrap and diving in where the fighting was at its fiercest?
It's true that on the mean streets of Glasgow back in the late 1930's, his quick temper had got him into many a tight corner as the scars on his be whiskered face and mangled ears bore unquestionable testament to. These had been scary times when he had taken on more than he could chew and it was in such circumstances that his phenomenal turn of speed had come in handy. On more than one occasion he had been seen outpacing his pursuers through the back alleys round the Gorbals.
It was on one such desperate flight that he had met up with Jock McCue. With at least half-a-dozen adversaries hot on his heels, Scottie had scaled a backyard wall and leaped from the top, right into the arms of Jock, who was making his way to the privy at the bottom of the little yard.
"Steady on there boy, you're shaking like a leaf. Is someone chasing ye?" As if in answer to the question Jock heard the raised and angry voices of Scottie's pursuers as they dashed past the backyard wall, their cries gradually diminishing as the angry pack raced on in vain pursuit of their target.
"Och mon, ye're nobbut skin and bone," cried Jock as he comforted the still shaking intruder. *"When did ye last have a good square meal?"* Scottie made no reply and yet the rumble from his stomach told Jock all he needed to know. *"Well I can feed you this once but ye'll have to go to wherever your hame is after yer done laddie."* Jock was as good as his word and Scottie was treated to probably the best meal he had eaten for many a long while. He was just

about to settle down for a snooze when Jock reminded him of his earlier pronouncement and politely but firmly escorted him to the backyard door.

"Now it's nay gud yus looking at me like that; ye canna stay. We're crammed in like sardines as it is. I'm hame on leave and even I hae to sleep on a camp bed. Come on now, shape up laddie." Jock peered out of the back door before announcing, *"The coast is clear - off ye go now – and try and keep yerself oota trouble."*

Reluctantly Scottie retreated from the shabby but welcoming house and wondered when he would ever dine so lavishly again. Still he had long since become accustomed to the harsh realities of fending for himself. He had been turned out of his home at an early age and had been living and eating rough ever since. It had started to rain as Scottie made his way to the smoke-stained railway arches. At least it would be dry there and with a bit of luck he could get his head down for a few hours at least.

Dawn was just breaking when Scottie was rudely awakened from his slumbers. Standing over him was the leader of the gang who he had so narrowly evaded the previous day. Other members of the mob were also in close attendance and Scottie knew that this confrontation would not end happily. The early morning Glasgow to London express passed overhead, making just enough noise to distract the pack momentarily. It was all that Scottie required and with a twist of his lithe and sinuous body he leaped over his startled antagonists and once more found himself fleeing for his life, as if pursued by all the hounds of hell.

Whether by luck or sheer coincidence, he found himself passing the same alleyway where he had found such welcoming sanctuary the previous day. Could he push his luck once again? He realized he had little choice, the pack were hard on his heels and with a prestigious leap he found himself once more in that same dingy backyard. *"Nae, not you again?"* It was Jock. This time he was dressed in his army fatigues and was busily applying a military shine to his already glistening boots. *"I guess you'll never be oot o' trouble while you're living round here – but I think I know how we can fix that; come on now laddie and follow me..."*

The training had been intensive and Scottie was not the most attentive of recruits. Despite his apparent indifference to army life it was not long before he had revealed that his one natural attribute was his turn of speed and when he was in full flight there was not a 'squaddie' on the camp who could catch him. However, Scottie had not settled easily to military style life and the seemingly unending discipline. For all his short existence he had been a free spirit and taking orders had not been easy for him. However, on the plus side there had been a regular supply of food, a warm place for him to rest his head each night and best of all the constant companionship of his new found mentor Jock, who had managed to persuade the recruiting sergeant to place Scottie with him in his own platoon. The pair were now pretty much inseparable.
It came as no big surprise when in 1944 the battalion learned that they were to join up with the rest of the

brigade for the big push by the allies up through mainland Italy. It was not long after landing that Jock and Scottie saw their first action. Their infantry platoon was to the rear of the advancing troops, engaged in mopping up operations when from the ruins of a small farmhouse, which less than an hour ago had been in enemy hands, they heard the distinct sound of a military radio – and the message coming from it was undoubtedly in German. They were fortunate that the young lieutenant leading the men was fluent in the language. As he listened to the urgent voice of the sender his face paled. He raised his hand to ensure absolute silence from his men and within minutes the message ended with those chilling words – Heil Hitler!

"My God," he exclaimed, his face ashen. *"Their artillery forces have pinpointed the position of our advance troops and at 1400 hours will open up a barrage on them. By that time they will be in open country with no chance of cover. It will be total carnage."*

"Can wi no get a message to them to retreat back towards the hills," queried Jock. *"Unfortunately not, our field radio was damaged in that last little skirmish with the Krauts; we have no way of getting a message to them in time; it's almost 1330 hours now,"* replied the lieutenant.

"We could always send young Scottie. If anyone can deliver a message in time it's him."

"He'd never make it. The whole area is a nest of machine gun emplacements and snipers – It would be suicide."

"Sir, ye dinna have much choice but to give it a go." With reluctance the young officer agreed. The hastily scribbled

note was soon in Scottie's safe keeping and with words of encouragement from Jock he set off on his mission.
The rat-a-tat-tat of machine gun fire and the whine of the sniper's bullets announced to his comrades that he had been spotted – and a silent prayer was sent to the heavens from a dozen anxiously beating hearts...

"And so, on behalf of the regiment, it gives me great pride and satisfaction to award you with this special honour."
Jock nodded to Scottie who obediently lowered his head as the colonel bent to place the medal round his neck. If he had been able to read the inscription he would have seen that it said;

'FOR GALLANTRY – WE ALSO SERVE.'

He would also have noted that the medal displayed the initials PDSA. It was of course the Dickin medal, awarded for conspicuous gallantry or devotion to duty while serving or associated with any branch of the Armed Forces.
There was little doubt that Scottie truly deserved the medal as he trotted proudly around the barrack square, a sentiment that Jock and the rest of the regiment would no doubt heartily endorse. He was without doubt the bravest Scots Terrier that they were ever likely to meet!

Proof

37701322R00102

Made in the USA
Charleston, SC
14 January 2015